GIRL

VS

BOY BAND

THE
RIGHT
TRACK

GIRL VS BOY BAND

THE RIGHT TRACK

HARMONY JONES

BLOOMSBURY
LONDON OXFORD NEW YORK NEW DELHI SYDNEY

With special thanks to Lisa Fiedler

Bloomsbury Publishing, London, Oxford, New York, New Delhi and Sydney

First published in Great Britain in June 2016 by
Bloomsbury Publishing Plc
50 Bedford Square, London WC1B 3DP

First published in the USA in June 2016 by
Bloomsbury Children's Books
1385 Broadway, New York, New York 10018

www.bloomsbury.com

Bloomsbury is a registered trademark of Bloomsbury Publishing Plc

A CIP catalogue record for this book is available from the British Library

ISBN 978 1 4088 6854 6

Printed and bound in Great Britain by CPI Group (UK) Ltd, Croydon CR0 4YY

1 3 5 7 9 10 8 6 4 2

To my agent, Susan Cohen, with gratitude

CHAPTER ONE

Home is where the grass is green and just a little bit blue,
And there's no place in all the world I'd rather be, it's true.
If home is where the heart is ... if that's what people say,
Then mine is far away from you and breakin' every day ...

Lark Campbell's fingers moved gracefully over the strings of her beat-up old Gibson guitar. Every lyric she sang, every chord she played, had come from somewhere deep inside her, and now the sound of her music flooded the backyard just like the California sunshine.

Her favorite boots—distressed brown leather embroidered with dainty blue and yellow flowers—glided through the lush grass as she walked in time with her song. As a warm LA breeze ruffled the ends of her long auburn hair, she tilted her face toward the sky and belted out the final lines.

I can't feel the rhythm, and I can't hear the rhyme.

*What's a girl supposed to do when she's homesick all the
  time?*

"Cut! Beautiful!"

Lark opened her eyes and smiled at her best friend, Mimi
Solis. "Really? It was good?"

"It was beyond good," Mimi assured her. "It was
incredible."

Lark's cheeks flushed bright pink. "I'm not sure about
that last lyric, though. Maybe I'll change—"

"Don't change a thing!" Mimi dashed across the lawn
toward Lark. "Take it from the world's leading seventh-grade
Latina filmmaker—"

Lark laughed. "I think you mean the world's *only* seventh-
grade Latina filmmaker."

"Even better! I'm a true original. Just like this song."

Lark couldn't agree more; Mimi really was one in a
million. Lark had known that the minute they'd met on the
school bus eight months ago, back in sixth grade. Lark had
clambered onto the giant yellow vehicle, convinced there
was nothing worse than switching schools midterm. As
she'd made her way down the narrow aisle, not a single kid
offered her a place to sit. Then Mimi, in the very back seat,
smiled and waved.

"There's room here," she'd said.

Lark had sat down beside her, relieved. But before she could even introduce herself, Mimi was holding her phone in Lark's face, saying, "You just gave me a great idea for a documentary film. I'll call it *The New Kid: A Middle School Exposé.*"

"Um . . . okay," said Lark, feeling sick to her stomach.

It must have shown on her face, because Mimi gave her a sympathetic laugh. "Don't worry. Nobody'll see it. Except maybe my brothers, if I force them to watch it. I don't have much in the way of distribution just yet."

When all was said and done, the documentary turned out to be just a bunch of silly segments of Lark and Mimi becoming friends. But because it had been Mimi's goal of becoming a filmmaker that sparked their friendship, Lark had vowed she would always be supportive of Mimi's dream.

Now Mimi grabbed the sleeve of Lark's worn denim jacket and dragged her toward the pool. "Ya know," she said, dropping into one of the wrought iron chaise longues, "I've always considered myself more of an indie film kind of gal, but since you and I have become biffles, I'm thinking I might have a real future in directing music videos." To prove it, she twisted the video display so Lark could see it and hit the Play arrow.

A close-up of Lark's face filled the tiny screen, and she immediately felt her skin prickle with goose bumps. It was like being hit with a tidal wave of self-consciousness.

She snuck a glance at Mimi, who was watching the video with a critical eye.

The music through the miniature speaker sounded tinny, but Lark couldn't help thinking that despite the poor audio quality, the song sounded pretty great.

"Hmm . . . maybe I can add some special effects in the editing process," Mimi murmured thoughtfully.

"Can you make me look like any less of a dork?" Lark said, cringing at the sight of her face on the screen.

"Oh puh-leese," Mimi said. "Those perfect cheekbones, pouty lips, and zillion-mile legs don't need any improving! Girl, you are an album cover waiting to happen!" She turned up the volume and swayed her head to Lark's singing. "Talented *and* pretty—I'd have to hate you if you weren't my best friend."

Lark felt a tingle of gratitude at her friend's compliment. She'd spent most of her childhood feeling like an ugly duckling. Even though her mom always assured her that she'd grow out of her gawky shyness, Lark wasn't convinced that she was a swan in the making.

Mimi paused the video, backed up a few frames, and hit Play again. "I really like this moment, when you're half in the shadow of that orange tree. Very moody."

"Who knew citrus had such screen presence?" Lark teased, sitting down on the chaise next to Mimi. She leaned back and cradled the guitar, loving the way the golden-yellow wood looked against the faded indigo of her jeans. Her new kitten, Dolly, skittered over from where she'd been hunting in the shrubbery and leaped onto the chair to settle against Lark's hip. Absently, Lark began strumming a few bars of "Homesick," wondering if perhaps it should be a little more up-tempo. She knew if she just let her fingers linger on those strings, sooner or later the answer would come to her.

She had a newer and fancier guitar upstairs in her bedroom, which overlooked the pool. But this one suited her much better. It felt familiar, like an old friend. It had been her dad's guitar when he was her age. He'd given it to Lark back when she turned twelve . . . a month before her mom gave *him* the divorce papers. She could remember her mother's voice, floating into her room from the kitchen.

I love you, Jackson, she'd said. *But you're gone so often, sometimes I feel like we're not even a family anymore.*

I have to travel for work, Dad had reminded her. *That's what session musicians do, Donna. We go on the road.*

Lark's mother had sighed. *I need to do something bigger with my life than just shuffling papers at some tiny Nashville record company and waiting for you to come back from a tour. Lark needs more, too.*

Lark remembered wanting to burst into the kitchen and tell her mother she was wrong—she didn't need more. The only thing she needed was what they already had. But her mom's next words had stunned her, freezing her in place.

I'm moving to the West Coast, she'd said. *I'm starting my own record label and it's going to be ten times the size of Rebel Yell. And I'm taking Lark with me.*

Dad had put up an argument, but even Lark knew it was a fight he couldn't win. She would have been overjoyed to stay in Nashville with her dad, but his unpredictable schedule would make that completely impractical. It just didn't make sense for a kid her age to be traipsing around the country, tagging along after her father with a guitar slung over her shoulder . . . no matter how much she would have loved it.

Eventually, her dad was forced to agree that Lark belonged in California with her mother. It was the first time Lark had ever seen her dad—who usually only expressed his emotions through his music—cry. Lark had felt her heart split in half that day.

Mimi sighed, jarring Lark out of her memories. "Your song is amazing, and I want the video to be really good, too," she said. "I want to do something that will really grab the viewer's attention."

"Whoa . . . ," Lark said nervously, sitting upright. "I don't *want* to attract attention. I don't want anybody to see this video except for you." Lark had agreed to let Mimi film her so that she could hone her filmmaking skills, but Lark was so shy that Mimi had had to promise to keep the videos secret.

"Don't worry," said Mimi, shaking her head emphatically. "I'd *never* show our videos to anyone without your permission. I just want to capture the essence of the song. Ya know—wholesome country girl with a heart of gold, stuck in the big city . . ."

"Um, thanks." Lark bit her lip. "I think." She knew Mimi meant it as another compliment, but the description made her sound like some hillbilly who'd just fallen off the back of a turnip truck.

Mimi put down her video camera and flopped back on the lounger, her arms spread wide as if waiting for inspiration to strike. Turning her head to squint at Lark in the late September sunlight, she asked, "Are you really, truly *that* homesick for Nashville? I mean, I know it must be hard to be away from your dad, but I can think of a few very cool things Los Angeles has that Nashville doesn't."

"You?" asked Lark, grinning.

"As a matter of fact, yes," said Mimi. "And let's not forget the one and only Teddy You-Can't-Get-Him-Out-of-Your-Head-y Reese! The most crushable boy in our whole school."

Lark rolled her eyes but she didn't dispute it. She'd had a crush on Teddy since the moment she first saw him, and nobody knew that better than Mimi. Actually, nobody knew that *except* Mimi.

"You just got back from spending practically the whole summer with your dad in Nashville," Mimi reminded her. "Didn't that help at all?"

Lark closed her eyes and pictured some of her favorite moments of the summer. A night out with Dad at the Grand Ole Opry; an afternoon on the shady front porch, listening to his Loretta Lynn and Dolly Parton records like they did when Lark was little; a deliciously spicy dinner at Prince's Hot Chicken. (Her tongue was *still* burning!) "I reckon it did help while I was there," said Lark. As always, thinking about home caused her Southern drawl to become more pronounced. "But now that I'm back here, I feel like a stranger all over again. I know LA is beautiful, and I'm lucky, but I'd gladly trade this fancy house and swimming pool for my dad's cozy little place in Nashville. Sometimes the homesickness is so deep, I feel like I'm drowning in it."

"*Drowning* in it!" Mimi jumped up from the lounge chair, frightening furry little Dolly, who let out a tiny mew of annoyance. "That's it! *That's* how we can make the video more interesting."

"What is?"

Mimi jerked her thumb toward the glistening blue pool and grinned. "Sink or swim, girlfriend! You said it yourself . . . you're *drowning* in homesickness."

"Drowning?" Lark gasped, horrified. "Hey, now, Meems . . . I totally get suffering for your art and all, but I don't think I'm willing to go *that* far."

Mimi laughed. "Lark, I don't mean you have to *actually* drown. Duh! Who would I eat lunch with at school if you did that?"

Lark knew better than to protest when her friend had an artistic vision. The last time they had made a video together, Mimi had convinced her to paint her face camouflage-style and sing with her head poking out of a shrub. Lark had been doubtful, but had to admit the video was pretty cool. Her best friend was kind of a genius. It was a shame nobody ever got to see their music videos, but that was the deal.

Half an hour later, Lark was lying on a pool float, fully clothed. "I can't believe I'm doing this," she grumbled. As she shifted her weight to get more comfortable, water spilled over the edge of the raft and soaked her jeans. "Ugh! This feels gross."

Mimi, who was standing on the diving board in full-on director mode, smiled down at her. "You know you love it! Now, let your hair just kind of sprawl out around you, mermaid-style. Perfect! I think we're good to go. Let me just hand you your guitar—"

"No!" Lark sat up so fast, she nearly toppled off the raft. "Don't bring my guitar anywhere near the water!"

Mimi frowned, but only for a second. Then she snapped her fingers, and her face lit up. "No problem. You can sing a cappella in this shot. It'll add some variety!"

Lark lowered herself back onto the plastic float. The sun was scorching, but the gentle rocking of the raft and the lapping sound of the clean, clear pool water were soothing.

"Action!" called Mimi as she hit Play on the track they'd recorded on her phone the week before.

"If home is where the heart is, if that's what people say . . ."

Lark sang and drifted, trailing her fingers over the cool surface of the water, impulsively splashing up a slender arc of glittering spray during the chorus. She lost herself in the floating and the lyrics and the music of her own voice.

"I can't feel the rhythm, and I can't hear—"

The sound of the patio door sliding open startled Lark so much that she slipped off the raft and into the water. Her heart was pounding as she came up for air.

"Lark!" came her mom's voice. "Why are you swimming in your clothes? You'll ruin your boots!"

Lark pushed her dripping hair away from her eyes and climbed out of the pool, her sodden jeans hanging heavily off her hips. "Tell me about it," she muttered as she squished across the patio.

Lark's mom looked at the girls suspiciously. "What on earth are you girls doing?"

Lark shot Mimi an urgent look. On the list of people Lark *didn't* want to see her perform (and that included pretty much everyone on the entire planet except Mimi), her mother was at the very top. Since the divorce, she and her mom hadn't been getting along very well. Lark's songs were about her deepest feelings, and she definitely didn't want to share them with her mom—whom she still blamed for making her leave Nashville.

Mimi, as always, could read Lark's expression and knew exactly what she was thinking. She had already turned off the track and snapped the screen shut. "I dropped my camera case in the pool by accident, and Lark jumped in to rescue it for me," Mimi said.

Lark's mom seemed to buy Mimi's explanation. She tottered on her stilettos across the patio and handed Lark a towel, then sat down at the table. "I've asked Mrs. Fitzpatrick to bring out a pitcher of sweet tea."

"Nice to see you still like some Southern things," Lark said tightly.

"Oh, the tea is for you girls," said Donna, waving off the dig. "I'm having coconut water."

"Of course," Lark muttered. She wrapped the towel around her soggy clothes and sat down across from her mother, who looked as polished as ever in her tailored business suit and flawless makeup. Back when they lived in Tennessee, her mom had worn jeans and boots like everyone else. Lark missed her dressed-down mom, the one who liked to go hiking and didn't work late all the time.

The one who hadn't needed to live in a house that was three times the size of the one they'd shared with Lark's dad when they were still a family. But Donna had explained that in many ways the music industry was all about appearances, and if she wanted to be treated like an LA music mogul, she'd need to look the part. So she'd rented some office space downtown and had the words Lotus Records painted in silver on the glass door. Then she'd invested in a new business wardrobe for herself and taken out a lease on this enormous house. Lark thought it was all ridiculously phony. Two people rattling around in all these empty rooms, just for show! But her mom insisted it would pay for itself in no time. Unfortunately, the plan was beginning to backfire. Although everyone in the business agreed that Lotus was an up-and-coming label, it was still in the growth phase, and the profits were taking much longer to add up than Donna had anticipated. Although she hadn't come right out and told Lark they were heading for financial trouble, Lark was smart enough to know that money was tight, and getting tighter by the minute. Her mom needed a hit band . . . and she needed one fast.

When Mrs. Fitzpatrick bustled over with the refreshment tray, Lark noticed she'd included a plate of fresh-baked cookies. The matronly housekeeper smoothed her apron, which read, I'd Tell You the Recipe, But I'd Have to Kill You, and she watched expectantly as Lark helped herself to a cookie.

"Mmm," Lark said, nibbling tentatively. "Chocolate and . . . something else?" There was another flavor in the cookie that she couldn't quite place.

Mrs. Fitzpatrick nodded, her tightly permed gray curls bobbing. "Chocolate and avocado," she announced proudly. "I noticed some ripe avocadoes on the trees outside and popped them in the mix. I thought they'd add vitamins."

Lark finished her cookie and gave Mrs. Fitzpatrick a thumbs-up. Smiling broadly, the housekeeper bustled back into the house. Mrs. Fitzpatrick was always trying out new recipes. Even though chocolate and avocado sounded like a strange combination, it somehow worked—unlike the peanut-butter-and-marmalade cookies she'd baked earlier in the week.

"Why are you home so early, Mom?" Lark asked, reaching for another cookie.

"Because I have news," said Donna, sipping her coconut drink. "Big news."

Mimi gulped down a mouthful of tea. "You guys aren't moving back to Tennessee, are you?"

Lark held her breath. *Are we?*

"No, Mimi," said Donna, grinning. "Lark and I are here to stay."

Lark's heart sank.

Her mother pulled a tablet out of her briefcase. "I want to talk to you about a music video."

At that, Lark almost gagged on her cookie. Had her mom somehow found out about the videos she and Mimi had made? The thought filled her with horror. It would be like her mom reading her secret songwriting journal, but worse.

But when her mom clicked on a link, Lark relaxed.

"I want you to watch this and tell me what you think," said Donna. "You too, Mimi. I'd love your thoughts, since you're so creative."

Mimi, whose own parents were more much more interested in her grades than her artistic endeavors, glowed under the praise. It was moments like this, when her mother could be genuinely nice, that Lark felt guilty about being so resentful all the time.

Donna handed the iPad to Lark, who hit Play.

Three boys in their teens appeared as the intro to a song began. They were in a park, it seemed, and at first they were just horsing around, throwing friendly punches, showing off some dance moves. Two of them were dressed in jeans and T-shirts; the third wore all black, right down to his combat boots.

After a minute or two, the music faded into the background, and the boys turned to the camera in unison.

"Hey," said the tallest of them in a British accent. "We're Abbey Road. I'm Ollie."

As the camera zoomed in on his blue eyes, Lark couldn't help but gasp. The boy was gorgeous. Shaggy blond hair, a rugged jaw, and lips that looked so ripe for kissing, they made Lark blush.

The next boy, whose brown arms had muscles to spare under his fitted T-shirt, waved at the camera, then did a standing backflip with ease. "I'm Max." His green eyes sparkled as he added, "As in maximum velocity."

"As in maximum hottie-ocity," Mimi whispered to Lark.

The camera then swung around to the third boy, the one in black. His hair was also jet black, and his cheekbones looked as though they'd been carved by a master sculptor. He wore black jeans, a black T-shirt, and a black leather jacket. As he raised his chin in greeting, his eyes glinted in a way that left no doubt that he was the group's "bad boy."

"That's Aidan," Ollie explained, poking his grinning face into the frame. "Moody bloke, Aidan is."

"Oi!" called Aidan playfully. "Watch it!"

The boys exchanged high fives.

"Let's get on with it, then," said Ollie.

The three boys launched into a pop song. It was catchy and upbeat; Lark found her toes tapping on the wet patio tiles. She'd never been one to fall for pop stars, and she'd always considered boy bands to be silly—moderately talented cuties who looked good on posters and merchandise. But as Abbey Road danced and sang, she couldn't help being impressed. These dudes could really *sing*!

Occasionally, the video would cut away from the park to the boys playing instruments in what looked to be a dirty back alley. Lark suspected Mimi would call the alley segments "self-consciously artsy," but being a musician herself, Lark found she liked the song even better knowing the boys could play their own instruments. She could tell from their technique that they were actual musicians rather than just eye candy miming along to someone else's playing.

"What do you think?" asked Donna when the video ended. "The song's called 'Dream of Me.'"

Mimi spoke first. "The video's pretty cheesy," she said honestly. "They made it themselves, right?"

"Right," said Donna, "but I'm talking about the band. What did you think of the boys?"

"Oh . . . ," said Mimi with a crooked grin. "Well, what I think is that I'd really love to get their phone numbers."

Donna laughed. "That's what I was hoping to hear." She turned to Lark. "What do you think, honey?"

"I think they've got talent," said Lark. "Ollie has a great range—he can even sing falsetto."

"That's what I like best about them," her mother said, nodding. "They've all got fabulous voices."

"To go with their fabulous looks," added Mimi.

"A winning combination," Donna agreed. "Which is why I've signed them to Lotus Records."

Mimi's eyes lit up. "So I *can* get their phone numbers! Maybe I can even invite them to LA for the weekend!"

"You won't have to," Donna said.

Lark lifted one eyebrow. "What do you mean?"

Her mother took a sip of her coconut water. "A British talent scout I know told me he'd seen these boys perform at an open-mike night in London. He said they were unpolished but had lots of talent and might be worth a look. So, while you were in Nashville this summer, I went to London and signed them. Now I'm bringing them here, and I'm going to make them huge stars."

Lark's heart pounded. "Bringing them *here*?" she repeated. But before she could ask her mom exactly what she meant by that, the patio doors slid open again and the housekeeper poked her head out.

"Mrs. Campbell, how many of the guest bedrooms did you want me to make up?"

"All *three* of them," Donna answered, then turned a big smile to Lark. "Abbey Road arrives at LAX tomorrow afternoon. So why don't you change into some dry clothes and help me get things ready."

CHAPTER TWO

Lark wondered if she was stuck in some kind of nightmare.

The airport was bad enough—the crowds, the heavy security, the departures board mocking her with posted flights to Nashville. Part of her just wanted to hop on the next plane to Tennessee and leave LA behind forever. Not that there would be much point in that; her dad was on tour playing rhythm guitar for a hot new country band and wouldn't be home for three months. Lark knew this was a major gig for him, but she couldn't help wishing she at least had the option of going home. It would be so nice to know her father was there waiting for her if she needed him.

But no, he was touring and she was stuck here in La-La Land, being jostled by a sea of travelers and holding an oversize poster-board sign complete with glitter-sprinkled bubble letters, which read:

AMERICA LOVES ABBEY ROAD!!!
WELCOME SUPERSTARS OLLIE,
AIDAN, AND MAX!!!!!

It was ridiculous!

Lark had outgrown glitter *and* bubble letters back in the fourth grade. But worse than both those things was the fact that the message on the sign was a complete lie. Superstars? Please! America didn't even know who Ollie, Max, and Aidan *were*, let alone love them. And since her life was about to be turned upside down and inside out to accommodate these three British strangers, it was Lark who loved them least of all.

Even if they were sort of talented.

Okay, and gorgeous.

But still . . . *glitter*? Come on!

"It's working," Donna whispered. "See? People are looking."

"I'm very aware of that," Lark muttered, feeling her cheeks burn red as passersby paused to scrutinize both her and her goofy sign. Her discomfort was compounded by the fact that her stomach was growling; her mother had rushed her out of the house without lunch.

"That's how the public is, honey," said Donna. "They all want to feel like they're in on something fabulous, like they could be the first ones to know about the next big thing."

Lark knew her mother was right. People were starting to linger around them, glancing toward the baggage claim in search of Abbey Road, who, apparently, were on the verge of big-time fame. A few of these looky-loos were punching "Abbey Road" into their smartphones to find out exactly who Ollie, Aidan, and Max might be.

Search all you want, you won't find anything, Lark warned them silently. *These guys are still nobodies.*

"Can't you please try to look excited, Lark?" begged Donna. "You're supposed to be waiting for your favorite British boy band to arrive. Let them see that gorgeous smile of yours. Or even better, giggle!"

Lark had sworn off giggling around the same time she'd gotten over the glitter thing. But she did manage to appease her mom with a passable imitation of a smile.

"Thanks, baby girl. I want you to look like a devoted fan. We're creating a mood here."

"Creating a mood, perpetrating a fraud . . . whatever."

"Sweetheart, this is how the business works," said Donna. "You know I'm trying to drum up publicity, and at the moment, I don't have the budget for anything more sophisticated than this."

Lark felt a wave of guilt. There was a great deal on the line, and she knew her mother was under a lot of pressure to make this band a hit. "Okay," she said. "What do you want me to do?"

"Scream or jump up and down or *something*—ooh! I have a better idea!"

Donna whipped out her phone, tapped the music app, and slid the volume up as high as it could go. Suddenly, the angelic but flirty voices of her new clients singing "Dream of Me" filled the baggage area.

People stopped in their tracks, turning to see what would happen next. Lark realized they were probably expecting a flash mob. She only wished that were the case—then she could get lost in it.

But the pop tune was working its magic. People began to tap their feet and nod along with the beat. Lark couldn't blame them; even through a cell-phone speaker the song was a crowd-pleaser.

"Go on," urged Donna. "Sing along!"

"*What?*" Lark almost dropped her sign.

"I know you know the song. I was playing it in the car the whole ride over and I saw you mouthing the words."

"But Mom—"

"Honey, won't you please help me out and sing?"

A bolt of panic shot through Lark's body. "Are you crazy? Here? In front of all these people?"

"Don't be shy. Please, won't you act like a real fan and sing along?"

"There's the problem. I'm *not* a real fan." Lark gave her mother a desperate look. "Can't we just wait for them to get here and let *them* sing it? It's *their* song." She peered anxiously toward the baggage carousel. "Where are they, anyway? They couldn't have stopped to sign autographs since nobody knows who they are yet. I can't believe they're keeping us waiting like this. That is so rude."

"Don't change the subject," said Donna. "You've got a beautiful voice. If you start singing, you'll get everyone's attention."

"Exactly!" cried Lark, her stomach flipping over.

The upbeat little pop number was nearing its bridge. Admittedly, the lyrics were clever and the tune was catchy, and although it had been written for teenage boys to sing, it was surprisingly perfect for Lark's own voice. She had been humming "Dream of Me" in the car, and halfway to the airport she'd started wishing she'd written it herself. For Lark, that was the sign of a great song—one she liked enough to want to claim as her own.

"Lark, please. I'm putting a lot of energy into making these boys a hit. Anything we can do to help that process along will be good for all of us."

Lark gripped the corners of her cardboard sign, her palms sweaty, her stomach roiling. She knew her mom wouldn't give up, and if Lark flat-out refused, Donna would grumble about this missed opportunity for days . . . or weeks . . . maybe even the rest of their lives.

So she swallowed hard and waited for the breathy, boyish voices to reach the song's chorus.

Do you dream of me when the nights are long?
When the world is dark, do you hear this song?

Singing in a crowded airport was definitely not Lark's idea of a good time. Out of the corner of her eye, she could see that the onlookers were really enjoying the music. She had to hand it to her mother—the woman knew how to create a commotion.

You're a dream come true, baby, don't you see.
My only dream is that you dream of me.

Lark closed her eyes, preparing to belt out the next line, but she was suddenly so light-headed she couldn't remember what it was . . . something about "sweet dreams," or "dream girl"? Her knees buckled but somehow she managed to stay on her feet.

Dream a little sweeter, dream a little more.
Dream of me, girl, like you never did before.

She opened her eyes, forcing the words to the tip of her tongue. Under the harsh airport lights, the world wavered, spinning in slow motion as she spotted a boy in tattered blue jeans and a snug white T-shirt sauntering toward the baggage carousel. Even through her blurring vision, Lark recognized him: Oliver Wesley, also known as Ollie, Abbey Road's front man and lead vocalist. With his tousled blond hair and piercing sapphire-blue eyes, the boy had "pop star" written all over him.

"Now, Lark!" Donna whispered as Ollie approached the baggage claim. He looked so cool and confident, unlike Lark, who had begun to tremble. What if she hit a sour note? What if she forgot the words, or her voice somehow betrayed her?

Ollie was so impossibly good-looking, Lark wondered again if she *was* dreaming. His presence was causing even more of a stir than the music had. Around her, young girls were gasping and pointing.

How was it possible that the simple act of tugging a suitcase off a conveyor belt could be making Ollie's already impressive arm muscles bulge like that?

But the bigger question was this: why wasn't she singing? She was *trying* to sing . . . here . . . now . . . in Los Angeles International Airport, of all places. She was making an effort, but something was horribly wrong. As far as Lark could tell, her mouth was opening and closing, but no actual *singing* was taking place.

"Where are the other two?" asked Donna, her tone on the

verge of panic. "Oh, Lord, please don't tell me they missed the flight! Or did we somehow miss *them*?" Hurrying off, Donna called over her shoulder to Lark, "Stay put. I'm just going to check the other side of the arrivals area."

Lark felt the poster board slip from her perspiring fingertips just as Ollie turned his dazzling face in her direction. When her wide-eyed gaze met his, a slow smile spread across his gorgeous face.

Dream a little sweeter, dream of what you feel.
Dream of me tonight, baby, dream until it's real ...

Lark's brain screamed the message to her vocal cords and she willed the lyrics to her lips.

She searched for her voice.

Instead, she found the airport floor.

Lark felt the cool tiles of the terminal floor against her spine; someone was gently patting her cheek.

Ollie?

She opened her eyes slowly, but instead of the British boy, she saw the concerned face of a security guard. Crouched beside him was an older lady, who was taking her pulse.

"Easy, there," said the woman. "I'm a retired doctor. Just making sure everything's still ticking."

Her calm voice and kind smile made Lark feel a bit better, although she couldn't understand why this stranger was fussing over her.

"Think you can stand up, miss?" the security guard was asking.

"Hmm? Oh . . . I don't know. I'll try."

Lark's attempt to gain her feet set the world spinning again. "I guess not," she sighed, lying back again. "What happened to me?"

"You must have passed out when that good-looking kid smiled at you," the security guard explained, and winked.

"*What?!* No!" Lark frowned. "He had nothing to do with it! If I fainted it was only because . . . because my mother wanted me to sing and . . ." She trailed off, her face turning red at the thought of the doctor and the security guard assuming she was the sort of girl who would go weak in the knees at the sight of some British hottie in his tight T-shirt and jeans.

"Nothing to be embarrassed about," the doctor said. "Same thing happened to me the first time I saw Elvis Presley on the *Ed Sullivan Show*."

Despite the haziness in her head, Lark smiled; as a Tennessee girl, that particular Memphis boy was practically a god.

"I love Elvis," Lark murmured.

"Do you, now?" The doctor grinned. "Well, ordinarily

when I check for a head injury I ask the patient if she can tell me her name and address, but perhaps I should ask you to sing me a few bars of 'Love Me Tender' instead." She chuckled, not expecting Lark to actually listen to her.

Maybe it was the wooziness that had Lark so relaxed, but before she could stop to think about where she was and who might be listening, she closed her eyes and began to sing the legendary ballad.

She breathed in to begin another line, but to her surprise a slightly deeper, sweetly familiar voice was already singing it.

Lark's eyes fluttered and for one crazy instant, she half imagined that the late, great King of Rock and Roll had returned from beyond the grave to serenade her. The lilting mystery voice joined with hers in perfect harmony.

As the notes faded to silence, Lark opened her eyes again and this time found herself staring up into Ollie's grinning face.

"I always love a duet," he teased. "But why is my singing partner sprawled on the floor?"

The security guard chuckled. "She took one look at you, kid, and she was swept right off her feet."

Lark could feel her cheeks burning. "That's not what happened at all!" she protested, struggling to sit up. "My mother wanted me to sing 'Dream of Me,' but I get nervous about singing in front of people. I've never been able to perform in public. I have terrible stage fright. This isn't even the first time this has happened to me. I fainted once before . . . Y'all don't believe me? I can prove it! I still have the scar on my forehead from the fall."

"Now, now," the doctor soothed. "Calm down, dear. Breathe."

Lark knew it would take more than a few deep breaths to overcome her anger, especially with Ollie smiling down at her with such a cocky expression.

The doctor and the security guard gingerly helped Lark to her feet, holding on until they were sure her legs wouldn't give way.

"I'm fine now," Lark insisted. "Thank you for your help."

The security guard grumbled something about paper-work and incident reports. "Are you an unaccompanied minor, miss, or are you here with your parents?"

"I'm with my mother," said Lark. "At least I was. Her name is Donna Campbell and—"

"Donna is your mum?" said Ollie. "Well, that explains it." He turned to the guard. "She's our manager's daughter," he explained. "I bet they faked this whole scene to show how crazy our fans are about us."

"You don't have any fans yet," Lark snapped.

"Fans?" said the guard. "So this whole thing was a publicity stunt? The fainting? That little duet? Which was very entertaining, by the way."

"And extremely romantic," the doctor added.

"Thank you," said Ollie, grinning.

Ewww, thought Lark.

But since the last thing she wanted was to spend an hour in the airport security office filling out an incident report, she nodded. "Yup, that's exactly what it was," she fibbed. "A publicity stunt. I just pretended to faint."

When the doctor and the guard were gone, Ollie picked up the glitter-encrusted sign and laughed. "Donna doesn't waste any time, does she?"

"No, she doesn't," muttered Lark, scanning the area. "Where is she, anyway?"

"With my mates."

Ollie pointed toward the baggage carousel, where Lark saw her mother. She was talking animatedly to another security guard, who stood frowning between the two other members of Abbey Road . . . who were both in handcuffs!

CHAPTER THREE

Lark and Ollie hurried toward the baggage carousel. From the way Ollie's cheeks dimpled with amusement, Lark got the distinct feeling he wasn't at all surprised that his bandmates were in trouble.

"I can't imagine what these boys have done to wind up in handcuffs," Lark's mom was telling the guard, "but whatever it was, I give you my word: from this moment on, they will behave like perfect gentlemen."

"Wouldn't count on that," Ollie whispered.

"Shhh!" Lark scolded. She was furious. The boys had been on American soil less than ten minutes and they were already causing mischief.

And then, suddenly, Max burst out laughing. He lifted his hands in front of his face and with a loud "Abracadabra," yanked his wrists apart. The cuffs fell away as if they were made of paper. Aidan grinned and did the same.

Donna blinked. "What in the world . . . ?"

"The bloke we sat next to on the flight happened to be an illusionist," Max explained, still laughing. "He's here for some magicians' convention. We told him we'd let him backstage at our first concert if he let us borrow his trick cuffs. Pretty funny, eh?"

The guard gave Donna a sheepish smile. "The boys talked me into going along with the prank," he confessed. "They're very charming kids, as I'm sure you're aware, so I couldn't bring myself to say no. They said their new manager would get a real kick out of it."

"Kick out of it?" barked Donna, her eyes flashing. "They nearly gave me a heart attack!"

The guard's smile faded and he flushed with embarrassment. "If you folks will excuse me, I've got to hurry along. Just heard over my walkie-talkie that some teenage girl passed out."

Ollie let out a snort of laughter, and Lark shot him a warning look.

"Thank you, officer," said Donna, looking relieved.

Only now did Lark notice that the crowd who'd assembled to hear "Dream of Me" had completely dispersed. Not a single onlooker remained in the vicinity to witness the handcuff trick. She was sure her mother had cleared the area the second she'd spotted her protégés being escorted by law enforcement. How she'd managed it, Lark could not imagine, but she knew that her mom would *never* allow anything even remotely resembling bad publicity to tarnish the up-and-coming band's reputation.

And now that it was clear that the up-and-coming band in question wouldn't be spending the rest of the day in jail, Lark relaxed and took a moment to study the boys out of the corner of her eye.

Aidan was rubbing his un-cuffed wrists. He was dressed from head to toe in black—mostly leather—just as he'd been in the video. Even though he'd been part of the joke, something in his expression told Lark he wasn't as naturally lighthearted as the other two. He had a mysterious, brooding air about him.

Max, on the other hand, with his broad smile and warm green eyes, seemed to think the whole world was a good time just waiting to happen. "Still sulking?" he said to Aidan now, throwing a friendly elbow to his bandmate's ribs. "I can't help it if that girl who was flirting with us the whole flight turned you down when you asked for her number."

Ollie laughed. "That 'girl' you're talking about was the flight attendant, who was probably twice your age. And she wasn't flirting with any of us; she just was doing her job."

"She gave me an extra bag of pretzels," Aidan pointed out with a wink.

Donna pursed her lips impatiently. "I'm sure she thought you were all adorable. But this kind of thing simply can*not* happen. Traipsing around in handcuffs is *not* going to get you to the top of the charts."

"Loads of rock stars have served time," Ollie quipped. "Mick Jagger, Paul McCartney . . ."

Lark rolled her eyes. Did he really think this was funny?

"Let's get the luggage," her mom suggested. "The sooner we put this nonsense behind us, the sooner we'll be on our way to making you three the world's next big teen sensation."

As Aidan and Max followed Donna, Ollie turned to Lark. "I wonder what they'll think when they hear I made the first pretty girl I saw in LA faint."

"They won't think anything," Lark seethed. "Because they'll never know. Understand? Not one word to my mom, your 'mates,' or any other living soul, because—"

Lark stopped walking. Had he just called her a pretty girl?

Yes, he had.

She scowled. So on top of being cocky, Ollie was sarcastic, too. Great. Just great. She shook the thought out of her head and tromped onward. "Just keep the fainting to yourself."

Ollie laughed. "I'll take it to the grave," he promised. "By the way, what's your name?"

"It's Lark."

"Lark!" Ollie's eyes lit up. "Well now, that's fitting. You're quite the little songbird."

Lark felt her heart speed up. That's what her father called her . . . his songbird. For some reason, hearing her nickname from this smug British hottie made her even angrier than she already was.

"Just get your bags," she huffed. "I want to go home."

"Right," said Ollie, lifting his carry-on over his shoulder. "Home to Beverly Hills!"

Home to Nashville, Lark corrected silently. *The sooner, the better.*

The boys threw their bags into the rear hatch of the SUV. Ollie, clearly the group's leader, opened the driver's side door.

"Wrong side, you numpty," said Max, chuckling.

"Oops, I forgot you guys drive on the right," Ollie said with a grin, going around to the passenger side.

"You definitely don't want Ollie to drive," Aidan said with a laugh. "He totaled the go-cart we built together a few years back."

Since Lark was the smallest, she had to ride in the backseat, sandwiched between Aidan and Max. As they drove down the freeway, her mom pointed out all the sights and landmarks, as proudly as if she'd been born and raised in LA. The Hollywood sign especially excited the singers.

Lark's anger had given way to an extreme sense of discomfort. She didn't have a lot of experience with boys, and now here she was sitting between two terrifically talented ones with another in the front seat, all of whom (if her mother had anything to say about it) would be pinned to the walls of teenage girls' bedrooms all over the world in less than six months. This thought made Lark laugh—the boys themselves wouldn't be pinned to the walls, of course . . . just their pictures.

"What's so funny?" Max asked, smiling at her.

The friendly overture took Lark by surprise.

"Oh, I was just thinking about something," she answered, unwilling to admit she was imagining their faces on posters.

"Was it dinner, by chance?" Aidan asked, rubbing his belly. "I'm famished."

"I've got a wonderful meal waiting for us at home," said Donna.

"Wicked," said Max. "But don't go to any trouble on our account. We eat anything from curry to bangers and mash."

Lark had no idea what a banger was, but imagining her mother preparing it—or any other actual meal—had her laughing again. Back in Nashville, her mom had cooked all the time—good, old-fashioned "stick to your ribs" Southern meals, and Lark and her father had reveled in the comfort of sitting around the kitchen table to enjoy them. Of course, that had all changed when Donna Campbell launched the Lotus Records label. She was much too busy with the uphill climb of launching a fledgling record label to find time to cook.

And when there was time, she was simply too exhausted. Mrs. Fitzpatrick, the housekeeper Donna had hired to keep an eye on Lark after school, was an adventurous cook, but Lark still missed her mother's home cooking. Especially as some of Mrs. Fitzpatrick's attempts at global cuisine were less than appetizing. Lark crossed her fingers and hoped that the boys never mentioned "bangers and mash" in front of *her*!

"How old are you?" Max was asking now, eyeing Lark. "Thirteen?"

"She's twelve," said Donna pointedly. "Only twelve."

Lark blushed. The unspoken subtext of her mother's words was a very firm *much too young for you*.

Max nodded. "I thought so. I've got a little sister who's nearly thirteen. You remind me of her. She has a great laugh, too. Ollie's got two brothers. His older brother's some sort of genius—going to Oxford next year."

"He got the brains, I got the looks," Ollie said, making a funny face and crossing his eyes comically.

"Do you have any siblings, Aidan?" Donna asked.

"Nope—it's just me," Aidan said. "I guess my mum and dad knew they'd achieved perfection first time round."

"Or they didn't want to risk having another moody bugger like you," sniggered Max.

"Lark's an only child, too," said Donna. "Do you find it lonely, Aidan?"

"This lot are constantly round my house, so I don't have much opportunity to feel lonely," Aidan said.

"It's because your house is amazing. Aidan likes to come off tough, like he grew up on the mean streets of London, but really, his family's dead posh." Max dragged a hand through his mop of dark curls and laughed. "I'm the only one from the wrong side of the tracks."

Lark couldn't tell if he was joking about that. Their British accents all sounded posh to her. She considered their different backgrounds. "So how did you guys find each other?" she asked.

"Well, Max and Aidan met in prison," Ollie quipped.

Donna shot Ollie a stern glare. "Oliver, I know you're only trying to be funny, but it could be misconstrued. Fans will be documenting your every move. They'll record everything you say in public."

"So what if they do?" Aidan said. "Ollie's just being cheeky. None of us have been to jail."

"Yet," Max whispered to Lark with a grin.

"Regardless," Donna said. "The press would have a field day with a comment like that."

"What do you mean?" asked Ollie.

"The minute your career takes off, the media is going to start searching for the skeletons in your closets."

"If they find any in Aidan's, I'll bet they'll be dressed in black leather," Ollie joked.

Aidan leaned over the front seat and smirked. "You're just jealous because I'm the one who's going to get all the attention. Girls always love the 'mysterious one' in a band."

"You're about as mysterious as a boiled egg, Aidan," Ollie retorted with a snort.

Aidan responded by giving Ollie a playful flick on the ear.

"Rule number one," Donna interjected loudly. "From this moment on, you boys are going to act like you're—what's that term you always use, Lark? Baffles? Buffles? Biffles!"

Lark groaned. "Please don't say 'biffles,' Mom. You sound ridiculous."

"Well, I don't care what you call it, as long as you get along. I promised your parents you'd stay out of trouble and I don't want to let them down. Understood?"

"Got it," said Ollie, sounding genuinely contrite.

The other two didn't reply, but Lark could tell that her mom had made her point. "So how *did* you get together?" she asked again.

"We went to the same school," explained Ollie. "We were in the same music class, but the stuff the teacher made us play was rubbish, so we started bunking off school to play music together instead."

"Our school was just off Abbey Road and we're all massive Beatles fans," Max added. "So that's how we got our name."

As her mother guided the SUV into the long driveway, Lark snuck a glance at Max. His eyes widened as the enormous, contemporary mansion came into view. She wondered what he'd think of her father's cozy house in Tennessee, with the creek in the backyard and the shady front porch. Or what he'd say if he knew Donna nearly burst into tears every time she wrote out a rent check for this place.

"You'll each have your own room," Donna said as they all climbed out of the SUV.

"Good plan," said Ollie as he helped the others unload suitcases and instrument cases from the back. "Might eliminate some of the bloodshed." He caught himself and offered Donna an apologetic smile. "Sorry. I promise that's my last joke." He carried a black guitar case to the front porch, then returned to the vehicle for another load.

Donna shook her head and smiled, and Lark realized that her mother couldn't help being charmed by Ollie's quick wit and clever banter. In spite of herself, Lark was warming to him, too. Maybe if he could rein in his overblown opinion of himself and edgy jokes long enough to keep from sabotaging her mom's plans for the band's success, Ollie might be fun to have around.

But as Ollie and his bandmates took the last few bags out of the SUV, he suddenly shouted, "I bagsie a room with a view of the pool!" and started sprinting toward the front door.

"Not if I beat you to it, mate!" called Aidan, chasing after Ollie with Max in hot pursuit.

Ollie had nearly reached the front door when Aidan tackled him from behind. A moment later, Max piled on top of both of them. The next thing Lark knew, all three boys were rolling around on the perfectly manicured grass of the front lawn.

"What's going on?" Donna shrieked. "Boys! What are you doing?"

Ollie had Max in a headlock; Aidan struggled to get to his feet but stumbled over Ollie's outstretched leg and crash-landed in the flowerbed. The one the landlord had specifically told them was custom-designed by LA's most sought-after landscape architect.

"Get off me!" Aidan demanded, laughing wildly as handfuls of stems and petals went flying into the air.

Suddenly, the air was pierced by a shrill whistle. All three boys and Lark and Donna whirled to see Mrs. Fitzpatrick, standing on the front steps of the house. She had the thumb and index finger of her right hand poked into her mouth; in her left hand she was holding a gorgeous Fender Stratocaster.

Lark's mouth dropped open, not only because she hadn't known her housekeeper could create a sound like that, but also because she'd never seen such a gorgeous musical instrument in her life.

Ollie looked up from the wrestling match and his face went deathly pale. "W-what are you doing with my guitar?" he croaked.

Mrs. Fitzpatrick turned the guitar so it gleamed under the porch light. "That all depends," she said, "on whether you young men are going to start acting like civilized human beings or not. If you are, then I will place this guitar carefully back into its case. But if you insist on shouting and wrestling, then I am going to smash this instrument into a million little pieces right here on the driveway."

"No!" cried Ollie. "Please don't. We were just playing. Blowing off steam after the long flight, you know." He scrambled out of the flowerbed, holding up his hands in surrender. "We were just messing around. I promise, we'll be more careful from now on."

"Very well." Mrs. Fitzpatrick nodded, smoothed down her apron that read, In the Kitchen, I'm the Boss, and went back into the house.

"I guess we'd better stay on her good side," Aidan observed, quirking his mouth.

"I'm going to go unpack." Max picked up his suitcase and headed inside. "Before she gets any ideas about my stuff."

Ollie took off after him. Aidan followed, leaving Lark and her mother alone in the driveway.

Donna was staring at the torn-up flowerbed in dismay. "We're going to have to pay for that," she muttered. Then she turned to Lark with an expression that didn't quite make it to confident. "It's been a long day. After they've had a good night's sleep, I'm sure they'll be fine." She gave Lark a forced smile. "It's going to be awfully exciting having them around, isn't it?"

"You can't be serious!" said Lark. "As if living in California weren't bad enough. Now we've got to share our home with *them*." Fuming, she turned and made her way to the house. When she reached the front steps, she turned back. "And don't ever ask me to sing in public again!" she shouted.

With that, she stomped inside and up the stairs to her room and threw herself onto her bed. She was clearly going to be spending a lot more time in here from now on—it was the only place where she'd be safe from *them*!

CHAPTER FOUR

Whoever said that teenage males were averse to grooming had obviously never lived with them.

Lark's three new housemates hogged the bathroom all morning, using up every last drop of hot water and leaving a trail of wet towels across the entire floor. By the time Lark finally got into the shower, there wasn't even enough time to wash her hair. Not that she could have done so anyway, as between them they'd finished all the shampoo! Evidently one of the boys had helped himself to Lark's blemish cream, because half of it was squirted all over the vanity.

When Lark arrived in the kitchen, she discovered that the Abbey Road boys had also eaten a whole box of cereal and polished off an entire carton of orange juice. Mrs. Fitzpatrick had fried a dozen eggs, but by the time Lark sat down at the table, they'd gobbled down every last one.

"They're growing boys," Donna said with a shrug. "But since the whole reason they're bunking here instead of in a hotel is to save some money, I wish I had factored in the expense of teenage boys' appetites."

"They're growing, all right," muttered Lark. "Growing more annoying by the minute."

Right now, the boys were taking selfies in their fancy new home. "Check this out," called Max, striking a funny pose in front of the huge television.

"Now take one of us," Aidan said, thrusting his phone into Max's hand. He and Ollie stood with their arms around each other's shoulders and made silly faces.

"Nice one," said Ollie, chuckling as he looked at the picture. "I'm going to send that one to my brother—he'll be dead jealous when he sees the pool in the background!"

Lark glared at the boys. For the first time since she'd moved to LA, she was actually looking forward to spending the day at school. Only now did it occur to her to wonder how the boys would be handling their education.

"Did you enroll the boys in school?" she asked her mother nervously. Setting these three loose on Beverly Hills High would give a whole meaning to the term "British Invasion."

"They'll have tutors," Donna replied. "And since they're going to be homeschooled, I'll need you to clean out the room over the garage when you get home. They can have their lessons in the kitchen for today, but starting tomorrow, that's going to be the school room and rehearsal space."

Lark felt anger bubble up in her chest. That room was one of the only things she liked about living in a house the size of the *Titanic*. "That's where I like to go to practice guitar and keyboard," she reminded her mother. "All my instruments are there. Not to mention that room has the best acoustics in the whole house." It was also far enough away that nobody could hear her sing.

"I know, honey. But we all have to make sacrifices if we want this to work," her mother said.

Lark bit back a sarcastic comment. It didn't seem like the boys were having to make a whole lot of sacrifices. Right now, the three of them were horsing around on the sofa. Max and Aidan were laughing hysterically as Ollie did an imitation of a teacher at their old school.

Glancing down at the calendar on her phone, Donna called the boys over. "Boys, when your classes are finished for the day, I'm going to have Mrs. Fitzpatrick drive you across town to meet with a stylist. Max, I think you're going to need a haircut. And Aidan, maybe we can introduce at least one additional color into your wardrobe?" She looked up from her phone to appraise Ollie, who grinned at her. "Ollie . . ."

"Yes?"

Donna studied him, then smiled. "Actually, you're perfect just the way you are."

Ollie's easy smile indicated that this was not news to him.

Lark rolled her eyes. "I'm going to be late," she huffed. "Has anybody seen my lunch?"

Aidan and Max both turned to Ollie, who held up a flattened brown bag. "Fitzy packed you a tuna mayo sandwich," he said with a guilty look.

"You ate my tuna sandwich?" Lark wrinkled her nose. "For breakfast?"

"I guess my stomach's still on Greenwich Mean Time," he said. "In London, it's lunchtime."

"Wonderful," said Lark. "So what am I supposed to eat when twelve o'clock noon Pacific Standard Time rolls around?"

Donna reached into her purse and pulled out a few dollar bills. "Buy lunch today, honey," she said. "I'm sure it will be delicious."

Lark wasn't sure of that at all. But she took the money her mother offered and headed off to the bus stop.

"Grilled cheese, please," said Lark, smiling halfheartedly across the chrome counter at the lunch lady. "Extra carrot sticks, no tater tots."

The lunch lady plopped the items onto a plastic plate, ignoring Lark's request to forgo the pseudo-potato pieces. Then she slid the plate across the countertop. "You get a dessert with that," the lady informed her. "Chocolate pudding or fruit cup."

"Neither, thanks," said Lark.

"Take the pudding," said Mimi, bounding up beside her. "I'll eat it!"

The lunch lady slapped a cup of slimy-looking pudding onto Lark's tray, then motioned for her to continue down the line to the cashier. Mimi was practically skipping along beside her as Lark paid, then they made her way to their usual table by the windows. They passed several signs for the upcoming International Fair.

"What's that fair thing all about?" Lark asked, sliding her tray across the table and taking a seat.

"It's fun, actually," Mimi explained. "Kind of a hands-on way of promoting diversity. Parents and grandparents come in and teach us about their different nationalities through cooking demonstrations and other kinds of cultural presentations. Mostly, it's a lot of really yummy food!"

Lark eyed her mushy grilled cheese. "Good to know."

"So . . . ," Mimi bubbled, "tell me everything! What are they like? Are they all stuck-up and snobby, or are they, like, normal and down-to-earth? I texted you a zillion times last night, but you never responded!"

"I know," said Lark, slipping into a chair. "I'm sorry. I was just so tired after the airport and moving the boys into their rooms and all, I went right to bed."

"'The boys,'" Mimi repeated, beaming. "You say that like you've known them forever! I still can't believe a real live band is crashing at your house. It's so cool."

"You know what's not cool?" Lark grumbled. "Fainting at the airport."

Mimi's eyes widened. "Tell me everything!"

So Lark gave her the CliffsNotes version of the sign, the song, and the swoon, cringing throughout the entire tale.

"Don't sweat it," Mimi advised. "It was probably low blood sugar. Now, back to the boys. Are they as cute as they looked in their video?"

"Cuter," Lark admitted, poking at her unwanted tater tots. "Especially Ollie." She bit into her grilled cheese, which was even soggier than she'd feared. "But they fight constantly. It's exhausting."

Mimi snatched the pudding cup and dunked a plastic spoon into it. "Yeah, that's how my brothers are. Willie is always trying to clobber Jake, and then Michael jumps in and it's a free-for-all. Nobody ever gets hurt, but it drives my mother crazy!"

"Mama chalked it up to their exhaustion and all," said Lark. "But I don't know. It felt like maybe there was something else going on. Something deeper."

"Deeper, huh?" Mimi gulped down the spoonful of pudding and reached for a tater tot. "Well, how were they to *you*? Friendly? Flirty? Or too full of themselves to even acknowledge your existence?"

"Friendly, I guess," said Lark. "But, Mimi, they're going to take over my music room for their homeschool classes. It's like I don't have any personal space in my own house." She dropped the disgusting sandwich back onto the plate. "They eat like there's no tomorrow and they hog the bathrooms and use all the hot water. If I don't die of hypothermia from taking freezing cold showers I'll probably starve to death."

Mimi laughed. "Now you know how I feel!"

"What do you mean?"

"I have three older brothers and one younger sister, remember? You've basically just described every single morning of my whole entire life."

Lark smiled. "I never thought about that before. Maybe your first film should be about life in a large family."

"Not a bad idea. Although I'm not sure whether it would fall into the category of screwball comedy or horror movie."

"C'mon," said Lark, biting into a carrot stick. "Is it really that bad?"

"Nah. You know I love my sibs. I guess that's the difference in our situations. You have to put up with a bunch of guys you don't actually love." She raised one eyebrow and grinned. "Or do you?"

"What?"

"Be honest . . . when you met the really gorgeous one . . . Ollie, right? Were there any sparks flying? Any soul-searing romantic moments when your eyes met his?"

"No!" cried Lark, feeling her cheeks flush. "And for the record, our eyes only met twice. First when I was half-unconscious, and then when he confessed to eating my tuna sandwich . . . so if there were any sparks flying, they were sparks of fury, not romance. Besides, they're all older than me."

"Not by that much."

"Still, it's hard to feel crushy about a guy who steals your zit cream."

"Ollie stole your zit cream?"

"Well, one of them did. I'm not sure who."

"I guess I see your point," said Mimi with a shrug. "Anyway, what would be the point, right? You've already got your crush." She smiled in the direction of the super-popular table, where Teddy Reese was offering a tater tot to a giggling Alessandra Drake.

Teddy was in eighth grade, which made him seem miles more sophisticated than Lark could ever hope to be. With his dark hair, blue eyes, and ready smile, he was by far the best-looking boy in school. It didn't hurt that he was also an honor student and the star of the soccer team. Mimi liked to say that Teddy was "the all-American boy, right out of central casting," whatever *that* meant. All Lark knew was that he was perfect.

Her face turned even pinker. "Teddy doesn't know I'm alive," she lamented.

"Well, I bet he'll take notice when everyone finds out you're living with the world's next super-hot boy band," Mimi observed. "Little advice? When that info goes public, you might want to leave out the part about the zit cream."

Lark laughed. "Yeah. Good call."

Mimi took another spoonful of pudding. "In other news, have you heard there's going to be a school-wide talent show next month?" She pulled a flyer announcing the contest out of her backpack and slapped it onto the table. "I was thinking maybe . . ."

She trailed off, shoveling more pudding into her mouth, but Lark knew a stalling tactic when she saw one. A feeling of dread welled up in her stomach, mingling with the gooey knot of undigested grilled cheese. "You were thinking maybe . . . *what*?"

"That I could enter one of my music videos," Mimi blurted. "And by that, I mean one of *your* videos. *Our* videos. I know it's not a traditional talent show act, but filmmaking is a talent and I'd love to be recognized for what I do. Nobody at this whole school knows I'm an aspiring director. It would be nice to get some props for a change."

Lark was seized by a grip of panic. "I totally get that, Meems, and I hate to have to be the one to point this out, but *you* being recognized means *I* have to be recognized, too. You know how I feel about singing in public."

"I know, I know," said Mimi. "I've heard the story a million times, all about poor little nine-year-old Lark Campbell, who was picked to sing "The Star-Spangled Banner" at the Nashville Fourth of July parade. But when she marched up to the stage in her adorable red, white, and blue sundress and opened her mouth to sing, she only got as far as 'the dawn's early light' before her head started spinning and she passed out. And she hasn't sung in public again since."

Automatically, Lark's thumb went to her forehead to trace the nearly invisible scar above her left eyebrow. "It was humiliating. I needed four stitches."

"It was three years ago!" Mimi put down the pudding cup and took both of Lark's hands in hers. "Please, Lark. If you let me use one of my . . . your . . . *our* videos, it wouldn't be like singing in front of a live audience. You wouldn't even have to be in the audience, although it would be cool if you were. Won't you just please think about it? Please?"

Lark looked around the lunchroom, trying to imagine what it would feel like to have her schoolmates hear her sing one of her original songs. The jocks, the cheerleaders, the cool kids, the fashionistas, the brainiacs . . . what would they think of her? Would they judge her?

Um . . . *yeah*, they would. This was middle school—of course they would judge her!

But what if they actually *liked* her sound? Maybe they'd say, "Wow, we didn't know the new girl was so talented."

Maybe Alessandra Drake—the best-dressed and most popular girl in seventh grade—would even ask where Lark got those cool, hand-tooled western boots she wore in every single video Mimi shot. Maybe Teddy Reese would think she had the sweetest voice he'd ever heard.

Or maybe they would they all laugh and call her a bumpkin for singing country music. Sure, country-pop was more mainstream than ever before, but she was an outsider, a Southern girl from Tennessee who idolized Dolly Parton and Kenny Chesney.

"I'll think about it, Meems," she said at last. "I swear, I'll think about it, but I can't make any promises, okay?"

Mimi nodded, then gave Lark a serious look. "It's not just for me, you know. You're such an awesome singer. You owe it to yourself to let the whole world in on the secret."

"Thanks," said Lark, her eyes darting to where Teddy was getting up to return his lunch tray. "I'll see what I can do."

When the bell rang, she told Mimi she'd see her later, in history class, then dumped the remaining ninety-five percent of her lunch into the trash and headed to the music room. It was time for her absolute favorite part of the day.

When Lark had first enrolled at school, she'd been placed in the standard music appreciation course, but it had quickly become clear that she could easily be teaching such a class.

When she'd refused to join concert choir or chorus instead, her advisor had suggested a special independent study in songwriting. Lark had been delighted by the opportunity; now three times a week she got to enjoy fifty-five private, uninterrupted minutes in the school's rehearsal room, strumming away on a guitar and composing original lyrics . . . all for class credit!

The rehearsal space was only a short walk from the cafeteria, and Lark always had to resist the urge to run there. Today she was especially eager to start writing; seeing Teddy Reese with Alessandra had filled her with envy, and she knew from experience how that could translate into moody lyrics fueled by genuine middle-school angst. But when she turned the corner toward the music room, she stopped dead.

Leaning against the door of her assigned rehearsal space—looking way too adorable for his own good—was Teddy Reese.

Lark wondered if she was having some weird reaction to the cafeteria food that was causing her to hallucinate.

No. Teddy Reese really was standing there, propped casually against the music room door. And from the way he was smiling, it was pretty clear he'd been waiting for her.

It was all Lark could do to keep from turning and bolting back the way she'd come.

"Hey," said Teddy.

"Uh . . . hey."

"You're Lark Campbell, right?"

Lark nodded.

"I'm Teddy Reese."

She managed to stop herself before blurting out an enthusiastic, *I know! Believe me, I know!* "Hi."

"I was wondering if I could ask you a favor," said Teddy.

Anything. Anything at all. Just name it. "Sure."

"Well, I take private voice lessons from Mr. Saunders after school some days."

"Really? From the choir teacher? Um, I mean, that sounds fun."

So Teddy Reese was a singer! If he'd been attractive before, he was downright irresistible now. Lark's heart swelled to think that she and this amazing boy actually had something in common.

"So . . . have you heard about the talent show?"

Lark nodded.

"Cool. See, I'm hoping to sing in it. Not sure what song yet, but I'm definitely going to sign up." He crooked a grin at her. "Mr. Saunders mentioned that you're an awesome guitarist and I was wondering if you were planning to perform in the show."

"No." Lark shook her head emphatically. "I don't think I can risk another head injury." The moment she said it, she wanted to kick herself. "Uh, I mean . . . I wasn't planning on it."

"That's too bad." When Teddy pushed away from the door and took a step toward her, Lark bit back a gasp. "Is there any way I could get you to consider it?" he asked.

For a second Lark was afraid this might be some kind of cruel joke, but Teddy's eyes seemed too kind for that. "W-what are you asking, exactly?"

Teddy's grin broadened into a smile. "I really like your accent. Where are you from?"

"Just outside Nashville," said Lark. "Tennessee," she added.

"Yeah." Teddy laughed. "I know where Nashville is."

"Oh, right. Of course. Sorry." Lark wanted to melt into the floor and disappear. Had she really just pointed out the location of one of the most famous cities in America? Now he probably thought she was some kind of idiot.

"Anyway," Teddy continued, "I was thinking maybe you could play backup for me in the show. Nothing too complicated, although from what Saunders says, I'm sure you could handle it. But I was just hoping for a little acoustic accompaniment."

Accompaniment. To Lark, that was suddenly the most beautiful word in the English language. "Me?" she whispered. "Play backup . . . for you?"

"Who better?" said Teddy.

"Pretty much anyone," Lark answered honestly.

"What do you mean?"

Lark took a deep breath. "I mean that unless there are going to be paramedics standing by, you probably don't want me onstage with you. I suffer from horrible stage fright. Singing in public is my biggest fear."

Teddy looked genuinely disappointed. "I was really hoping you and I could work together."

Why did he have to be so dang sweet? And why did she have to be such a wimp? Why couldn't she just find the courage to stand onstage and do what she knew she did so well? "I'm real sorry, but I just don't think—"

"Wait," Teddy interrupted. "You said 'singing' in public, right?"

"Yes," said Lark. "Singing in front of an audience sort of makes me . . . well, faint."

"Okay, but I'm talking about playing guitar. Just playing. No backup vocals at all. You wouldn't even have to hum." He gave her a hopeful look. "Are you afraid to play guitar in public?"

Lark thought about it and realized she had no idea. She'd never tried it. After that Fourth of July fiasco, she'd never allowed herself to set foot on another stage. So maybe she *could* play her guitar in public without winding up in the ER.

"I've never actually given it a shot," she admitted.

"So how about this: let's meet here on Monday after school and give it a try. By then I'll know what song I want to sing, and we can start goofing around with it. Just the two of us." He gave her a teasing smile. "And if that doesn't result in severe head trauma, maybe we can invite Mr. Saunders to sit in and watch, and you can see how that feels."

Lark couldn't believe how considerate he was being. The idea of performing still petrified her, but it was also clear that she didn't have it in her to refuse him this favor even if she wanted to. Not with his grin radiating excitement!

"Okay," said Lark, smiling back. "We can try."

Teddy pulled a pen and a folded sheet of paper out of his pocket. Lark recognized it as the talent show flyer Mimi had shown her at lunch. She had to catch her breath when Teddy printed their names side by side on the line labeled, Name(s) of Performer(s):

Teddy Reese and Lark Campbell.

She blushed, thinking of how many times she'd doodled those two names in the margins of her songwriting journal—of course when she wrote them there, they were usually enclosed inside a big heart. She'd even written a song or two about how much she liked Teddy.

"I really appreciate this, Lark," said Teddy, tucking the flyer back into his pocket. "So . . . I guess I should let you get on with your practicing."

"Okay."

"See ya."

"Bye." Lark watched as he headed down the hall, forcing herself to remember every nuance of what she was feeling, in the hopes that she might be able to put it all to music. Sensations becoming melodies, feelings becoming lyrics, heartbeats becoming rhythms. For her, it was the most natural thing in the world.

At the end of the hallway, Teddy turned back to smile at her. "So I'll see you on Monday?"

"Yes . . . Monday. Definitely."

"Excellent. It's a date."

The words echoed after him as he turned the corner. *It's a date.* That's what he'd said. *It's a date.*

Lark burst into the music room, aware of a joyful sound filling the space . . . a lilting ripple of laughter. It took her a moment to realize the musical sound was actually coming from her . . .

So maybe she hadn't completely given up giggling after all!

CHAPTER FIVE

Lark was so wrapped up in the song she was writing (not to mention her amazement at having had an entire conversation with her crush) that she didn't even hear the class bell announcing the end of fifth period. This resulted in her running halfway across school and skidding into sixth-period history four and a half minutes late.

"Thirty more seconds and that would have been a detention, Ms. Campbell," the teacher pronounced impatiently.

"Sorry, Mr. Corbin," Lark murmured, hurrying to her seat.

"Oh, it's not her fault she was late, Mr. Corbin," came a sweet voice from the seat behind her.

Lark turned and saw to her shock that it was Alessandra who'd spoken up on her behalf.

"And why is that, Ms. Drake?" the teacher asked.

"Well, she probably had to stop to rope a runaway calf on her way through the gymnasium," Alessandra said innocently, shooting a look at Lark's cowboy boots. "I mean, why else would anyone wear those hideous things?"

The whole class, with the exception of Jessica Ferris, Duncan Breslow, and of course Mimi, broke into hysterical laughter.

Lark lowered her head, wishing she could become invisible.

"Settle down," Mr. Corbin warned. "Open your books."

Lark's hands trembled with anger and embarrassment as she dug her history text out of her backpack.

"So what do you have next period?" Alessandra whispered from behind her. "Intro to Rodeo Clowning? Or is it Advanced Bull Riding?"

"Actually," Mimi snapped from the next row, "those happen to be totally unique, handmade boots. But you wouldn't recognize genuine style if it bit you on the nose."

To Lark's surprise, Jessica piped up. "I really like them." Then she gave Alessandra a grin. "But don't feel bad, Ally. Those sandals you're wearing are nice, too. In fact, my *grandma* has the exact same ones!"

Mimi let out a snort of laughter.

Alessandra's eyes flashed with fury.

"Ladies!" said Mr. Corbin. "That's enough."

As the girls opened their history texts, Lark saw Mimi give Jessica a thumbs-up and mouth the word "thanks."

Lark knew she should have been the one to thank Jessica (whom she barely knew) for having her back, but she was afraid that if she so much as made eye contact with Jessica—or anyone else—she'd die of humiliation.

Or worse, cry.

So she buried her crimson face in her history textbook and said nothing.

For the next fifty minutes, Lark tried to concentrate on the historical significance of Edward Braddock and the Seven Years' War, but her attempts were useless. Behind her, she could feel Alessandra's disgust wafting over her like a dark cloud, and she imagined that every time Mr. Corbin turned to face the Smart Board, every kid in the room was sneaking amused glances at Lark.

When at last the class bell rang, she sprang to her feet and dashed for the door, painfully aware of her angled heels clunking loudly across the floor.

On Monday, she resolved, she would thank Jessica for her support.

And she would definitely wear sneakers.

At home, Lark slammed the front door behind her and tossed her books on the foyer table. The weekend lay ahead, but that did little to cheer her up.

Is it just me, she thought, shucking off her beloved boots as though they had somehow become poisonous, *or does everyone feel like middle school is an emotional torture chamber?*

What she wanted—no, actually, what she *needed*—was to just drop herself into the overstuffed chair by the window of her music room with her guitar cradled close to her. She knew that the moment she felt those familiar strings against her callused fingertips, her whole miserable day would melt away like ice cubes in a glass of sweet tea on a hot Tennessee afternoon.

Does every seventh grader come home from middle school feeling like they've been hit by a truck, she wondered, *or is it just me?*

Despite her gloomy mood, Lark smiled. The thought sounded like the start of a lyric.

And besides, the day hadn't been a total disaster. Teddy Reese had spoken to her. Not just some random, mindless hi in the hallway, either. He'd sought her out, waited for her, and said nice things about her musical talent.

He'd said he wanted her to accompany him on her guitar.

He'd said, "It's a date."

So what if Alessandra Drake-the-Snake had made fun of her favorite boots? What did *she* know? Little Miss Granny Sandals.

Lark was feeling a zillion times better as she climbed the back staircase to the sprawling room above the garage. She was already composing a tune in her head when she pushed open the door.

And then it all came back to her.

Because there they were, in all their British glory, taking over her music room just as William Pitt's English forces had laid siege to Fort Duquesne in 1758. (Okay, so maybe she *had* understood some of what she'd read in history class. But that was *so* not the point!)

Ollie was lounging in Lark's comfy writing chair with a purring Dolly in his lap; his shoes were off and he was plucking the strings of her acoustic guitar with his big toe! Max was banging away on her electric keyboard (sounding terrific, given that he was the drummer, but also not the point), and she counted three different Victoria's Secret catalogs scattered about the carpet. Aidan was leaning against the wall flipping through her songwriting journal, and there was a half-eaten tuna sandwich in the middle of the floor surrounded by several empty soda cans and candy bar wrappers. And if that weren't bad enough . . .

Whoa. Wait a minute.

Aidan was flipping through her songwriting journal.

Feeling queasy, she flew across the room and snatched it out of his hand.

"What do you think you're doing?" she demanded, glaring furiously. "That's private."

"Donna told us to make ourselves at home," he said with a smile. "So that's what we're doing."

"Home?" She clutched her journal to her chest. "Then I guess y'all live in a pigsty, because that's what this place looks like."

Max's fingers halted on the keyboard; he glanced around the room and gave her an apologetic look. "We're supposed to be writing a new song, but Aidan and Ollie couldn't stop bickering long enough to accomplish anything." Then he turned to the others. "Lark's right," he said. "We're behaving like swine. Come on, guys. Let's show a little respect and tidy up." He reached for the sandwich and the soda cans.

Ollie gently nudged Dolly aside and started collecting the catalogs.

Aidan removed himself from the wall to assist with the cleanup. As he brushed by Lark to reach for a candy bar wrapper, he nodded toward the journal. "Good stuff," he said.

Lark didn't know whether she wanted to hug him or strangle him. And something told her this wasn't the last time she'd be feeling this way.

Ollie nodded to the chair he'd just vacated. "It's all yours, Lark. We'll go outside, maybe play a little football, and give you your privacy."

"No," said Lark, grabbing her guitar and feeling like a complete fool. "I shouldn't have yelled. I'll find somewhere else to work. You stay."

"Nah, don't go," said Max. "We weren't getting anything done anyway. Stick around and tell us what it's like to be an ordinary American kid."

Lark felt the words like a slap. Ordinary! Why hadn't he just called her plain and average? Thoroughly dull and completely insignificant!

She must have looked stung, because Max quickly shook his head. "I didn't mean that like it sounded," he amended. "I just meant—"

Lark forced a smile. "It's fine. I am ordinary. No big deal."

Max opened his mouth to dispute this, but suddenly all Lark wanted was to get away from there. She felt silly and out of place, which was ridiculous, since this was her house.

Is it just me, or do you feel this way, too?
I'm feeling so lost, like I don't have a clue.
Is it just me, thinking life's not on my side?
Is it just me, swimming against the tide?

Lark scribbled the lyrics onto a fresh page in her songwriting journal, silently lamenting the smudged chocolate fingerprint Aidan had left in the bottom corner.

She'd been locked in her room for nearly two hours now, and she had two good, solid verses to show for it. The page was dotted with notes, many of which she was sure would change a hundred times before she was through. She liked the melody for the most part, although she had a hunch it could be better. How exactly, she couldn't say, but she knew the solution would come to her eventually. She was sure of it. The best songs were always elusive to begin with, hovering just out of reach, teasing her until finally the melody revealed itself in a flurry of sharps and flats, key changes and rests. Musical notes that hadn't existed in precisely this order before would mysteriously come together, arranging themselves (with a little help from Lark) into a unique tune.

This song had a much more pop-y feel than her usual compositions, which were country through and through. But the bridge was giving her trouble and she wasn't sure where to go with it.

"Time for an expert opinion," she said aloud, putting down her guitar and reaching for her laptop. Minutes later she was listening to the mechanical singsong tones of a video call being placed, eagerly waiting for her father's face to fill the blank screen.

"Hey there, darlin'," came her dad's voice through the computer speaker.

"Hey, Dad!" Lark peered closely at the screen and laughed. "What's that you got on your face? Did y'all give up shavin' or somethin'?"

"As a matter of fact, I did." Her father chuckled and rubbed his scruffy chin. "Not by choice, though. It's for the tour. The band thinks the ladies might prefer me this way. They say it makes me look dangerous."

Lark had to admit that the stubbly, five-o'clock shadow was an excellent look for her already handsome dad. It took a second before she realized what he'd just said.

"Wait. *Ladies? What* ladies?"

To her father's credit, he looked a little embarrassed. "Ya know . . . the female fans."

Lark wrinkled her nose in disgust. She didn't like the idea of "ladies" having dangerous thoughts (or any other kind) about her dad. She knew her parents were almost officially divorced, but the thought of Jackson Campbell dating made it feel much too final. Dating *groupies*, no less!

"Well, it looks real itchy," Lark observed curtly. "I think you should get rid of it."

Her father, who knew her better than anyone, understood exactly what she was thinking. "Come on, now, Songbird," he said gently. "We've been through this. Your mom and I aren't getting back together."

"I know, I know." *But that doesn't mean I don't hate it.* "Anyhow, I didn't call to talk about your love life."

"Well, that's good, because at the moment I don't have one." Jackson smiled. "So what's up?"

Lark's reply was to play him her new song. When she got to the bridge, she shrugged. "I'm stuck. Any ideas?"

They spent the next half hour working as a team, her father far away—where was he, anyway? Chicago? Las Vegas? New York City?—strumming his guitar and making suggestions, and Lark, sitting cross-legged on her bed in LA dashing off notes, trying out chords, adding new lyrics.

They were just finishing up when she heard a loud thud, followed by a hoot of laughter just outside her door.

"What was that?" her father asked.

"Our new houseguests," said Lark, rolling her eyes. "Three teenage boys from England. They were probably horsing around and accidentally knocked a painting off the wall, or maybe one of them got cheeky and broke another one's nose."

This casual report had her father looking stunned. "Did you just say 'cheeky'?"

"Yeah. Sorry."

"I don't understand. Is this some sort of student exchange program for school?"

"Nope. They're a brand-new boy band Mama found in London. She just signed them to her label and now they're staying with us so she can keep a close watch on them and I guess save some money."

"Oh, really?" Dad raised an eyebrow. "So my little girl is living in a house with three strange teenage males who need to have a close watch kept on them?"

"Well, they're not *that* strange," Lark joked.

"You know what I mean, Songbird," her father said in a serious tone. "This feels like trouble waiting to happen."

"It's fine, Dad," Lark assured him. "They're too busy sniping at each other to even give me a second thought. As far as they're concerned, I'm like an annoying little sister. And besides, they really don't need all that much lookin' after. They might be a little mischievous, but I honestly don't think they're . . . ya know"—she paused, then grinned and rubbed her chin pointedly—"*dangerous.*"

Her dad laughed. "Touché, darlin'. Touché."

They chatted a bit longer about the grueling hours of the tour, Lark's schoolwork, and Mrs. Fitzpatrick's recent attempt at making Peruvian ceviche that was so sour, Lark's face puckered at the memory, then it was time for her dad to get ready for that night's show.

"Send me that song when it's finished, baby girl," he said. "I think it might be one of your best yet."

"Sure will, Dad. Love you."

He gave her a big wink, then he disappeared into cyber-space. Lark shoved the computer aside and played the song through with all her father's improvements. As the last notes faded to silence, she felt a tingle of pride and satisfaction.

"Is It Just Me?" was good. Bloody good, as the boys might say. She wondered what they'd think of it. Since the song was right for her voice, it would also be perfect for Ollie's. Smiling, she reclined into her pillows and sang the first line once more, attempting it (just for fun) with a British accent.

She was interrupted by a knock on the door.

"Come in."

To her surprise, Aidan poked his head around the edge of the door.

Weird, but seeing him like this—from just the neck up, without the distraction of all that black clothing—made her realize that he was almost as terrific looking as Ollie, with his pale skin and jet-black hair.

"Your mum sent me up to call you for dinner."

"Oh. Okay. Thanks."

She expected him to leave, but instead, Aidan cocked his head.

"What were you listening to just now?" he asked.

"Huh?"

"Just now. I heard music. Good song. Really good, in fact."

"Oh." Lark felt herself blushing. How long had he been listening outside the door? "That was . . . well, what I mean is, it *wasn't* actually . . ." She met his eyes, dark and piercing, and felt herself crumble. "Er, it was the radio. Just something on the radio."

Aidan gave her an odd look, as though he wasn't buying it, then disappeared back into the hallway and closed the door.

Lark sighed, reached for her pencil, and jotted down a new lyric to add to her song:

Sometimes I feel like I'm going kinda crazy.
Know what I'm sayin'? Or maybe it's just me.

CHAPTER SIX

Dinner was fish tacos with mango salsa. Lark supposed it was as good a compromise as any—not Southern, not British, but perfectly LA, which was home to all of them now. For the time being, at least. She also noted that Mrs. Fitzpatrick had wisely prepared enough to feed an army. Luckily, it was one of her tastier culinary creations.

"So," said Donna, draping her napkin over her lap. "How did the writing session go?"

"It didn't," said Aidan. "Ollie thinks his ideas are the only ones that count."

"That's because you didn't have any ideas," Ollie shot back. "I'm a better writer than you are; why can't you just admit it?"

"I would if you ever wrote something decent."

"Never mind," said Donna, holding up her hands in

surrender. "The songs will come. Every songwriter I've ever worked with has had days when the music just doesn't flow." Spooning some mango salsa onto her plate, she added, "Let's hope they come soon, though, as we've got studio time booked."

"Can't we ever talk about something other than your work?" Lark grumbled.

"Good idea," Donna said. "Let's get to know each other, shall we? I want to hear all about your personal lives back in England."

"Why?" asked Aidan, helping himself to a taco. "You're just going to have your PR people gloss over all the dodgy parts, aren't you?"

Donna considered this. "I guess it depends on how dodgy the dodgy parts turn out to be." She nodded toward Lark. "What sorts of things do you think your friends would want to know about the boys, honey?"

Well, *that* was a no-brainer! The one thing every fan—boy or girl—always wanted to know was if their pop star idols were romantically involved, and if they were, with whom. And if they weren't . . . well, that was the stuff daydreams were made of.

"They'd want to know if any of y'all have girlfriends," said Lark, biting into a spicy chunk of mahimahi.

"Of course." Donna eyed the boys. "So, do you? Aidan?"

To Lark's surprise, Aidan shot a death glare at Ollie and snarled, "Not anymore."

Ollie kept his eyes on his plate and said nothing.

"How about you, Max?" Donna asked. "Anyone special in your life at the moment?"

Max shrugged. "There was a girl from school I always sort of liked. We hung around together sometimes, but we never made it official. Her name's Lizzie. She's got red hair, big gray eyes. Clever, too. And she loves animals."

"Well, that explains what she sees in *you*," teased Ollie.

Max was so preoccupied in his memories of Lizzie that he didn't even seem to register the insult. "Haven't talked to her much since we got 'discovered.'"

He looked so homesick that Lark was reminded of the lyrics to her song. *Home is where the heart is . . . that's what people say.*

Now Donna turned her attention to Ollie. "And what about you, Mr. Wesley? Something tells me you're quite the heartbreaker."

At that assessment, Aidan snorted. "Heartbreaker? Try backstabber."

Ollie gave him a look that was a cross between fury and regret. "Not now, mate. If you haven't noticed, we're trying to have a nice dinner."

"Well, I've suddenly lost my appetite." Aidan narrowed his eyes and sprang up from the table, toppling the bowl of salsa.

Lark watched in amazement as Aidan stormed off.

So much for getting to know each other.

Saturday morning dawned warm and sunny. Lark was relieved to find that the beauty of the day seemed to banish all of the tension from the night before. At breakfast, Max and Ollie made all sorts of quips about never seeing the sunshine in England.

Even moody Aidan got in on it. "That explains why we're all so pale and pasty looking."

"Speak for yourself," joked Max.

Donna, who always slept late on weekends, arrived in the kitchen just as the boys were finishing the enormous pile of pancakes Mrs. Fitzpatrick had prepared.

"Big day, boys!" she announced. "You'll be meeting your choreographer this morning. His name is Jasper Howell and he had a hand in nearly all the dances at this year's Video Music Awards."

"Being he's a choreographer, I would think he had a foot in them, too," Ollie observed. "Maybe a couple of hips, a bum . . ." He gave his bottom a little shake.

Lark laughed.

"You know, I was planning to have you rehearse in the garage," said Donna, sipping from a tall glass of orange juice. "But you could use a little color in your cheeks. I think I'll have Jasper work with you outside instead."

Lark stopped laughing.

"Outside? You mean by the swimming pool?"

"Sure. There's plenty of space for them to learn their dance moves on the patio."

"But Mama, I've invited Mimi over to swim."

"No worries," said Ollie. "We aren't learning water ballet. You'll have the whole pool to yourselves."

Lark spun on her heel and headed for the stairs. The sense of panic was overwhelming. She was about to spend the entire day with LA's most sought-after choreographer and three gorgeous teenage boys.

And she was going to have to do it . . . *in a bathing suit!*

Mimi arrived at eleven o'clock, wearing a cute terry cloth cover-up and hot-pink flip-flops.

"What happened?" she asked, lifting her sunglasses to glance around Lark's bedroom. "It looks like a Lycra factory exploded in here!"

Lark was standing in front of her full-length mirror, studying herself with a critical eye. At the moment, she was wearing a navy-blue one-piece swimsuit with a V neckline and a scoop back. On the floor at her feet were two more bathing suits—another one-piece in bright orange and a red-and-white-striped tankini.

"I'm running out of options," said Lark, ducking into her

enormous walk-in closet to strip off the navy-blue suit and try on another. "None of these look right!"

"Please," said Mimi. "How could any of them look *wrong*? You've got, like, the perfect figure. I'd sell my video camera to have that tiny little waist."

Lark popped out of the closet, this time clad in a retro-style two-piece, with a high-waisted bottom and a modest halter top. It was her last suit.

"What do you think?" she said, looking over her shoulder to check out her backside in the mirror.

"Nice bloomers," said Mimi. "Very Marilyn Monroe."

Lark faced the mirror, glad to see that thanks to the cut of the suit, her belly button would not be making an appearance this afternoon. There was a great deal of bare back showing, but she could just about live with that.

"Since when are you so weird about bathing suits?" asked Mimi, gathering up the discarded swimsuits and dumping them into a drawer.

"I'm not weird, I'm just . . . conservative."

Mimi gave her a look.

"Okay, I'm shy." Lark sighed. "*Very* shy. And the idea of being so . . . um . . . well, *exposed* . . . in front of these boys— any boys, really—makes me extremely nervous."

Mimi laughed. "You are so old-fashioned! Must be a Tennessee thing. Now, c'mon, throw a hoodie and some sweatpants and maybe a blanket or two over that 1950s swimsuit of yours and introduce me to the band!"

With that, Mimi shed her cover-up, revealing a tasteful bikini with a gold clasp and ruffled trim.

"Take that, Tennessee." She giggled.

Grabbing her own cotton pool wrap, Lark followed her friend out of the room.

For the next hour, Mimi had the spotlight and handled it like a pro. Lark couldn't help but envy her friend's easy assurance and friendly, confident manner. It was as if Mimi had known Max, Aidan, and Ollie all her life.

Lark, on the other hand, got tongue-tied every time the conversation turned in her direction. She was back to feeling like a visitor in her own home.

After telling the boys all about her aspirations to be a movie director, Mimi asked them to describe their musical style.

"Pop with an alternative edge," Ollie explained.

"Rock with a nod to pop traditions," said Max.

Aidan said, "Loud. Our music's *loud*."

Mimi breezily segued into their lives in London. She wanted to know all about the city, especially the fashion and the arts scene.

"Cutting-edge," said Ollie.

"Always changing," Max noted.

"Loud," said Aidan again.

"I'd love to go to London someday," Mimi said, throwing Lark a grin. "So many amazing movies were filmed there. I want to visit James Bond's MI6 building, Sherlock Holmes's Baker Street, Harry Potter's Platform Nine and Three-Quarters . . ."

"I'd be happy to show you the sights," Ollie said. "London Bridge, Buckingham Palace, Big Ben . . ."

"Who's Big Ben?" Mimi asked. "A British rapper?"

Max cracked up. Ollie tried to hide a chuckle. Aidan just rolled his eyes.

"What?" asked Mimi.

Before Lark could explain, Jasper arrived and it occurred to her that she had never seen a more perfect specimen of humanity.

The A-list choreographer to the stars was young, about early twenties, and tall.

No, make that super tall. Six four, or maybe even six five. Muscular, with broad shoulders, long legs, and eyes the color of chocolate. He moved with such masculine grace and swagger that even his walk could be considered an advanced-level dance move.

"Wow," whispered Mimi as Jasper strode across the pool area to greet them.

"Hey, guys. I take it you're Abbey Road." Jasper gave the girls a friendly wave. "These your backup dancers?"

"Yes!" cried Mimi.

"No!" Lark blurted.

The boys introduced themselves and explained that Donna thought it would be best to hold the dance class outside. Jasper, or Jas, as he preferred to be called, was completely cool with that. He gave them a quick rundown of his career, which included working with some of the biggest names in music.

"Impressive," said Mimi. "And did I mention . . . *wow*!"

"So, let's see what you guys got," said Jas, looking around for a sound system and finding nothing. "Uh . . . gonna need some music."

"Right! I'll just go get my speakers," said Lark, happy to escape for even a moment. For the last sixty minutes, she'd been feeling self-conscious about everything from rubbing sunscreen on her legs to diving off the diving board. Right now she just needed five minutes to herself.

Ten would be better.

Invisibility would be best of all.

Wrapping her cover-up around herself, she hurried across the patio and slipped through the sliding glass door into the house. Her mother was at the kitchen table, finishing up a phone call.

"Jas is here," Lark reported. "I'm getting my speakers so they can get started."

"Excellent," said her mom. "But I've been thinking, honey. Maybe you and Mimi should leave the boys alone with Jasper for a bit. This is business, after all, and he might not want the band manager's daughter and her friend hanging around. Would you mind?"

Mind? It was like the answer to a prayer. Lark was just about to tell her mother this when Mimi burst into the kitchen.

"Grab your dancing shoes, girlfriend!" she cried. "Jas says we can learn the dance routines with the boys!"

CHAPTER SEVEN

"We'll start with a little freestyle to get warm," said Jas, placing his iPod into the speaker dock and hitting Play.

Ollie went first. He wasn't a bad dancer, but he wasn't what one would call a natural, either. He managed to keep time with the beat, but his moves were more athletic than graceful.

Aidan stepped forward next. "What do we have to dance for, anyway?" he protested. "We aren't some manufactured boy band. We're real musicians. We play instruments."

"Donna wants us to be the whole glossy package," Ollie reminded him. "The fans will like it. That means we'd better like it. So shut up and dance."

Aidan grumbled but did as he was told.

It was immediately clear why he was against adding dancing to the act. He couldn't stick to the beat and everything he did looked awkward and forced. Clearly, he would have trouble picking up Jasper's complex hip-hop moves. When Aidan finished his ungainly performance, he glared around at the group, as though daring someone to make a negative comment.

No one did.

And then it was Max's turn.

The second he broke into his routine, Lark gasped. She marveled at the way he was able to move in perfect sync with the music, sliding, spinning, even throwing in a little pop and lock.

"He's incredible!" breathed Mimi. "God, I wish I had my camera!"

Max finished with the backflip Lark remembered from their homemade music video, and everyone began to cheer.

"Well done, Maxie!" said Ollie, clapping his bandmate on the shoulder.

"Wow! But you're lucky you didn't bust your skull on those flagstones," Aidan groaned, but underneath the words, Lark heard his respect.

"We've got a lot of talent here," said Jas. "How about we try a combination? Guys, line up. Max, let's have you right here in front. Girls, come on, jump in. The boys need to get used to sharing the stage with backup dancers."

Mimi didn't have to be asked twice. She planted herself right next to Ollie.

Lark positioned herself a good three feet behind Aidan.

Then Jasper broke down the combination for them,

shouting out the steps and counting off the beats as he demonstrated. The boys followed his lead, as did Mimi and Lark. Ollie had some trouble with the turn at first, nearly tripping over his own feet, but he got it right on the second try.

"Okay, from the beginning," said Jas, reaching for the iPod. "Five, six, seven, eight . . ."

The music began to thump, and three handsome Brits, one lifelong Angeleno, and a very nervous Tennessee transplant started to dance.

"*Yeah,* baby!" said Jasper, snapping his fingers in time. "Yeah, that's it. Aidan, loosen up, dude. Ollie, stay with the beat. Mimi, nice attitude, girl. I love it! Max, you're doin' great. And Lark . . . perfect!"

Lark felt her cheeks burn, though whether it was from the praise, the exertion, or the hot midday sun, she couldn't say.

When they finished the combination, Jas gave them high fives all around, then told them to take a minute to catch their breath. Max offered to run inside and grab some water bottles for everyone.

"That was so cool," said Mimi, slipping a hair elastic from her wrist and wrangling her long mass of dark waves into a messy bun. "We're taking a dance class with Jasper Howell! If Alessandra Drake could see us now, right?"

Lark could think of nothing worse than being seen by Alessandra Drake, although she wondered if Teddy Reese would be impressed. After all, according to Jas, Lark's dancing had been "perfect."

But not as perfect as Max's, who'd returned from the kitchen and was handing her a chilled bottle of spring water.

"Thanks, Max," she said, twisting off the plastic cap and taking a long drink. "You're a real great dancer. Did you take lessons?"

"Nah. Lessons are expensive. I guess you'd say I'm self-taught." He took a gulp from his own bottle. "I just wish my singing was as good as my dancing."

Jasper clapped his hands. "Let's take it from the top, people."

The five dancers scrambled back into their lines and as the pounding beat filled the air again, they broke into their dance.

"Lookin' good," Jas said. "Use those shoulders. That's better. Energy, energy!"

The first eight counts were flawless. Lark could feel her heart racing as she slid easily from one step to the next. Max was showing off a little, and Aidan was just about keeping up with him. Mimi was smiling and singing along.

Then . . . it happened. And it happened *fast*! Ollie went into the turn with a little too much gusto. His ankle twisted beneath him and he went staggering into Aidan, who crashed into a chaise longue. Hard.

Furious, Aidan righted himself from the overturned chair and spun to face Ollie. "You utter pillock! You clumsy idiot!"

"Take it easy, mate. It was an accident!"

"Oh, it was, was it? Well, so's this!" Aidan's fist shot out and connected with Ollie's cheekbone.

"No!" cried Mimi. "Not the *face*!"

Ollie winced and swung back at Aidan, who ducked, evading the punch.

Lark felt herself being brushed aside as Jasper barreled past her to catch Aidan around the rib cage and yank him away from Ollie.

"Get off of me!" Aidan demanded. "Let me go."

Lark watched with wide eyes as the choreographer hauled Aidan across the patio.

"This is a dance class, not a street fight," Jasper said through gritted teeth.

"Bugger off!"

There was a shout, followed by a splash, and the next thing Lark knew, Aidan was coming up for air, gasping and sputtering in the shallow end of the pool.

"You just stay in there!" Jasper ordered, pointing his finger at the dripping Aidan. "Until you cool off."

Aidan gave him a wicked stare, but made no move toward the ladder.

It took a second for Lark to realize she was trembling. Unlike the play fight that first night in the driveway, this scuffle had been real. After the conversation about girlfriends, Lark had realized that the tensions between Ollie and Aidan weren't just down to jet lag or creative differences. There was definitely more to the story. Lark wondered if things were ever going to improve between these boys, or if the hostility between them was going to continue to escalate.

How in the world was she going to stand it if it did?

She turned to where Mimi was seated beside Ollie on a chaise, tenderly examining his bruised cheek. A slim trickle of blood was making its way from just beneath his eye to his chin.

"I don't think it needs stitches," Mimi observed. "But it's probably going to be black-and-blue for a while."

Lark looked from Ollie's injured face to Aidan, who was now floating on his back in the deep end of the pool: his black shirt billowed out around him, making him look like some sort of evil sea creature.

Then she turned to Jasper, who let out a long, disgusted rush of breath. Without a word, he headed for the house, presumably to tell Donna he was leaving and never coming back.

Only Max seemed unbothered by the madness. He stood patiently beside the speakers, looking as though nothing unusual had happened. When Lark caught his eye, he gave her a wry smile.

"All right, then," he said, reaching for the iPod's Play button. "Shall we try it again from the top?"

Somehow Donna was able to convince Jas to give the boys a second chance. They would meet again on Monday, this time at his dance studio, where he thought he might be able to exert a little more control.

Ollie had recovered from the fight quickly enough. Lark realized she liked this about him; he was generally an upbeat kid and didn't seem the type to wallow or sweat the small stuff.

Aidan, on the other hand, was turning out to be a sulker of the first order. After Jas left, he climbed out of the pool, dripped his way through the house, and stayed in his room right through lunch.

Mrs. Fitzpatrick carried a tray containing a big, leafy Caesar salad, and five frosty glasses of fresh squeezed lemonade to the wrought iron patio table. Crusty French bread and whipped butter came with the meal. It looked wonderful, but Lark wasn't in the mood.

"Come on," she said to Mimi. "Let's go to your house and see if we can talk your mom into making us her famous empanadas, then we can watch a movie."

"Are you nuts?" said Mimi, her eyes zeroing in on the empty chair next to Ollie. "I'm not going anywhere. What if something happens to Oliver while I'm gone?"

"Meems, it's a bruise. A few little scratches."

"Scratches turn into infections. Infections turn into comas! What if he died while I was off eating empanadas? I'd never forgive myself."

"Aren't you exaggerating just a bit?" said Lark. But she knew it was already too late. Mimi had a crush. Lark could tell because for some reason, whenever Meems *really* liked a boy, she started referring to him by his full first name.

"Besides, your mom said they were going to rehearse their new song after lunch. Oliver's singing lead vocals. I have to stay and hear it."

"Right," sighed Lark. "Because things went so well during dance rehearsal . . ."

But since Mimi was determined not to leave Ollie's—make that *Oliver*'s—side, Lark dropped into a chair and helped herself to some salad. With any luck, she'd develop some freak allergy to anchovies, break out in a horrible rash, and be forced to douse herself in Calamine lotion and spend the rest of the day in bed.

No such luck. The Caesar salad was delicious and then it was time for Abbey Road to sing.

They made their way up to the room formerly known as Lark's music studio. Aidan appeared in dry clothing (all black—big surprise) and glared at Ollie the whole time. The boys' instruments had been arranged and each boy took his place: Aidan at the electronic keyboard, Max behind his drums. Ollie picked up his Stratocaster as tenderly as if it were a newborn infant, which Lark fully understood.

She dropped cross-legged onto the carpet beside a dreamy-eyed Mimi, while Donna perched on the arm of the big chair.

First they played the song through once. It was called "Promises to Keep," and the composition was more sophisticated than Lark would have expected. But it was also infectious and fun. It was exactly the kind of tune that tween and teenage girls would adore—it would get stuck in their heads and they'd sing it off-key at the tops of their lungs on long bus rides to basketball games and cheerleading competitions.

Simply put, it had all the makings of a hit.

When it came time to try it with the lyrics, things took a turn for the worse.

Harmonizing, it seemed, didn't come easily to Max. He required a lot of coaching from Ollie, who was patient and polite. Aidan, though, grunted and rolled his eyes every time Max's attempts fell short.

"Max, maybe we should leave it alone for now," Donna suggested. "Ollie, you sing lead vocals, as we discussed, and Aidan, you sing harmony."

Max nodded, but Lark could see that he was disappointed. Maybe even a little embarrassed.

"Why does Ollie always get to sing lead?" Aidan demanded. "My voice is just as good as his. Why can't I sing lead?"

"Um, let's see . . . ," said Max, playing dumb. "Maybe it's because you look like the living dead, and fans generally don't respond well to love songs sung by vampires?"

"Shut up, Max," Aidan spat. "You can barely hold a tune. You ruined the harmonies."

"You know I'll get them eventually," Max shot back. "Just takes me a bit longer, that's all."

"Maybe we're tired of waiting for you to catch up!"

"Back off, Aidan," Ollie warned. "You know the only reason you're in this band is because of me! Don't make me regret inviting you to join!"

"That's right," Aidan sneered. "You *invited* me. But you *settled* for Max."

"Keep talking, Aidan," Max warned, "and you might find yourself with a drumstick somewhere you don't want it."

To Lark's horror, Aidan charged at Max and caught him in a headlock. But Max was agile; he spun out of it, and dodged Aidan's rocketing fist. Missing his target, Aidan stumbled. He slammed face-first to the floor, his nose hitting with a sickening crunch.

Blood began to gush.

"Ooooff!" said Ollie, cringing. "Right in the beak!"

Donna sprung up from the chair and quickly guided Aidan to the bathroom, frantically blathering about having to postpone photo shoots. A moment later she returned, clutching her car keys and looking harried. Aidan stood beside her with his head tilted back and a blood-soaked towel pressed to his dripping nose.

"We're going to the ER. I don't think it's broken, but better safe than sorry."

"I have an idea," said Ollie. "While you're at the hospital, why don't you see if you can have Aidan's bad attitude surgically removed?"

Lark had to bite back a giggle. Mimi laughed out loud.

Donna gave them each a sharp look. "This isn't funny," she scolded. "Lark, clean up, please. And Ollie, Max . . ."

Aidan let out a groan of pain as she nudged him toward the stairs.

"Keep working on those harmonies."

"Is she serious?" Ollie asked. "Here we are in the midst of violence and bloodshed, and she's thinking about videos and harmonies?"

"That's Mom," said Lark. "Business first. Always."

Ollie shook his head. "My mum would've been hysterical if she'd seen them scrapping like that. Which reminds me, I should probably ring her." He turned to Max. "Mind if I cut out for a bit?"

Max shook his head. "Nah, go ahead. And say hi to your mum for me."

Mimi got out her video camera. "Is it okay if I do some filming? There's more drama at your rehearsals than there is in an episode of a soap opera."

"No problem." Ollie gave Mimi his most charming smile. "You film me, if you like. For the archives."

Mimi was so delighted, she practically floated out of the room as she followed Ollie to the patio.

When they were gone, Max let out a heavy sigh. "Aidan wasn't too far off the mark, you know. I did mess up the harmonies."

"No, you didn't," Lark said, but it was halfhearted at best. He *had* struggled. So she summoned her courage and said, "If you like, I could help you work on them."

"That'd be brilliant," said Max. "Thanks."

They spent the next twenty minutes at the keyboard and Lark loved every minute of it. After the first few seconds, she wasn't nervous at all. She knew this was good practice for working with Teddy, which made it that much better. She instructed Max with patience, teaching him how to build up musical chords by blending their two voices. She used the same song her dad had used to teach her how to sing harmony, years ago—Elvis Presley's "Can't Help Falling In Love."

Max didn't once complain. He worked hard, and sounded better every time he sang it.

"I think you've got it," Lark said at last, just as Mimi came into the room.

"That sounded amazing. Maybe you should suggest that song to Teddy!" Mimi said with a knowing smile.

"Teddy?" Max gave her a sideways look and raised an eyebrow. "Who's Teddy?"

"Um . . ." Lark could have died! "Nobody."

"C'mon now," Max coaxed, smiling. "Have those lovey-dovey lyrics got you thinking about someone special?"

Lark shook her head emphatically, but of course Max was right. The line "Take my hand" had her imagining her own fingers entwined in Teddy's.

"Why not tell him?" said Mimi. "Maybe he can give you some advice."

Lark hesitated, but it suddenly occurred to her that it might feel good to share this with someone besides Mimi, perhaps even get a boy's perspective.

"Okay," said Mimi, reading Lark's mind, "so there's this boy at school . . . he's a year older."

She was interrupted by shouts of excitement coming from the pool area.

"I guess Mom and Aidan are back," said Lark, getting up from the piano and looking out the window.

She was right. They were back.

And they weren't alone.

CHAPTER EIGHT

"Is that . . . ?" asked Max, joining Lark at the window and going wide-eyed at the sight of the girl standing there on the pool patio.

It was Lark's turn to smile knowingly. "None other," she said.

"You never told me you know her!" said Mimi.

"You never asked," said Lark. "Wanna meet her?"

"Uh . . . *yeah*!" said Max.

They hurried outside, where Donna was introducing Aidan and Ollie to their surprise guest—Holly Rose, who just happened to be one of pop music's brightest new stars. Mimi had already whipped out her camera and was filming the whole scene. Ollie looked utterly enamored of the willowy blond singer and Aidan was staring like a smitten schoolboy.

It was still hard for Lark to wrap her head around the fact that the girl who used to visit their house in Nashville wearing cut-off jeans and vintage Oakridge Boys concert T-shirts was now the hottest thing in pop music. Donna and Jackson had discovered Holly Rose singing in a church choir five years earlier; she was just eighteen years old then, but her talent and sparkle were undeniable.

The small-town beauty had been thrilled when Lark's parents had approached her to make their business pitch: Jackson would coach Holly for a short period and when she was ready, Donna would bring her to the execs at Rebel Yell records to audition. After a mere three weeks of rehearsing on the Campbells' back deck, Holly was brought to Rebel Yell to perform. She was signed immediately, and despite the relative obscurity of the record company that released it, her first album went to the top of the country charts.

When Donna started her own company in LA, Holly proved her loyalty by ending her contract with Rebel Yell and signing with Lotus. Over the past year she'd crossed over from country to pop, with a string of hits.

It occurred to Lark now that Holly's success might be the only thing keeping her mother's company afloat. Still, one high-profile singer wasn't enough to support an entire business. Lark was suddenly filled with a sense of just how important it was for Abbey Road to make it big. But she didn't want to think about that right now.

"Holly!" cried Lark, running to greet her old friend with open arms. "I can't believe you're here!"

"Well, would ya look at you!" cried the superstar, catching Lark in a hug. "My word, I think you've grown six inches since I saw you last!"

"Only three." Lark beamed. "Well, maybe three and a half. But what are you doin' in Los Angeles?"

"Your mama flew me out. She wants me to record my new single here in LA. I just came by to play it for y'all, maybe see whatcha think of it." She gave Lark a wink and lowered her voice so that only Lark could hear. "Your daddy tells me your songwriting's getting real good, so I thought maybe you might give me a few pointers."

Lark felt a swell of gratitude; her father had remembered to tell Holly that Lark preferred to keep her songwriting secret, and Holly was respecting that.

"Lark, that's amazing!" Mimi whispered, aiming the camera to zoom in on Lark's beaming face. "Holly Rose wants *you* to help her with her song."

"That's right!" Holly laughed. "And girl, you *must* be getting good if you've got your own videographer!"

"This is my best friend, Mimi," said Lark. "Meems, meet Holly. She used to babysit for me!"

"Shut. Up!" said Mimi.

"No, really. Before she hit the big time, she used to take me to the park to go on the swings and—"

"I didn't mean 'shut up,' like I don't believe it," Mimi interrupted. "I meant 'shut up,' like actually *shut up* . . . I'm filming! This is great stuff. Big Nashville star meets up-and-coming British band. It could go viral!"

Max cleared his throat loudly.

"Oh! And this is Max," said Lark, continuing with the introductions. "He's in the band."

"Abbey Road," said Holly with a nod. "Yes, ma'am. Donna's told me all about these boys. Right down to that little brawl they just had." She grinned at Aidan. "No broken bones, I hope?"

"No, thank goodness," said Lark's mom.

Lark supposed this boded well for the band's imminent photo shoot. Black eyes and a bandaged nose wouldn't be an alluring look for an album cover.

Now Holly smiled around at the three starstruck boys. "It'll be a real pleasure sharing a label with you three."

"I wouldn't mind sharing more than that with you," said Aidan, leering at the pop star.

"Show a little class, Aidan," Ollie hissed.

Aidan ignored him and continued to make eyes at Holly, which was actually quite amusing, since he was forced to do it from behind the giant ice pack he had pressed to his nose.

"So let's hear the new song, Holl," said Donna. "The demo you sent me sounded great, but there's nothing like a live performance."

Only now did Lark notice the familiar old guitar case propped against the patio table. She knew it had once belonged to Holly's grandmother, who had taught Holly to play guitar, just like Jackson had taught Lark.

Holly took a seat on one of the chaise longues and began to play. To Lark's surprise, the song wasn't the feisty, up-tempo style of Holly's last few releases. This song was a ballad and Holly poured not only her voice but her soul into it as well. The lyrics were haunting and heartbreaking; Holly sang of missed chances, cherished memories, and lonely nights. Lark hazarded a glance at her mom during the chorus and was surprised to see a tear on her cheek. Was she thinking about Jackson, and all that they'd lost?

When the song ended, everyone applauded, but Holly's eyes went straight to Lark. "What do you think?"

Lark smiled. "I think it's awesome, but there're a few places where you could tweak the lyrics. It will sound even better with some harmonies, too."

"Please!" said Donna as she stood and headed into the house. "Don't say 'harmonies.'"

Holly patted the chaise longue for Lark to join her. "Well, let's get to work. I say we order in some barbeque and make an evening of it. Boys, let me know your thoughts."

When Aidan opened his mouth to make what was sure to be an off-color comment, Lark shocked herself by cutting him off.

"We don't need to hear what dirty thoughts *you*'re thinking, thank you very much," she warned.

They worked on the song until the sky turned a soft twilight purple, with Lark, the boys, and even Mimi throwing out suggestions. Rather than ordering in, Donna had Mrs. Fitzpatrick grill enormous rib eye steaks with roasted potatoes on the side.

After dinner, when Holly was finally satisfied with the changes to her song, they kept the music going by kicking off a good old-fashioned jam session. The boys ran upstairs and returned with their instruments. Ollie had his beloved guitar. Aidan had his keyboard tucked under his arm. Max was only able to bring his drumsticks, but he'd thoughtfully brought one of Lark's guitars down for her, as well. Then he cleverly fetched two empty chlorine buckets from the pool house and turned them upside down to create a makeshift drum kit.

Lark decided she would play, but that was all. Singing in front of a large group of people—even in her own backyard—was just too frightening.

Holly and the boys, Mimi and Donna, and even Mrs. Fitzpatrick, wearing an apron that said, Grill Sergeant, became an instant vocal group. They started by singing all of Holly's current hits, then they improvised on everything from old country standards like Hank Williams's "Your Cheating Heart" and Tammy Wynette's "Stand By Your Man," to the Beatles' iconic "Please Please Me" and "Come Together." Max even rapped a little. By the time Mrs. Fitzpatrick served the red velvet cake with cream cheese frosting she'd baked for dessert, Lark's fingers were tired and her cheeks ached from smiling so much.

She couldn't have been happier!

Then Mimi's father was honking the car horn in the driveway.

"Thanks for dinner," said Mimi. "And Holly, it was so great to meet you! I promise not to post any of this stuff on YouTube." She gave her a hopeful look. "That is, unless you want me to."

"I'd be grateful if you'd keep the new song under wraps for a bit," Holly said, "at least until after it's released. But you can put the other footage online whenever you want. I'd love my fans to see me rockin' out with these soon-to-be superstars!"

"I was hoping you'd say that!" said Donna. "I couldn't have asked for better free publicity for my two biggest acts."

When Holly stood up and reached for her ancient guitar case, Lark felt a tug at her heart. For the last few hours it was almost as if she'd time-traveled back to her childhood, singing outdoors with Holly on a warm night under the stars (minus three unruly British teenagers and the heated swimming pool, of course).

"Do you really have to go?" she asked.

"Sorry, hon, but I'm committed to a personal appearance at a club downtown. Your mama arranged it." Holly laughed. "I never in my life imagined I'd be getting paid big bucks just to show up at a party!"

Max turned to Donna with a grin. "When do we get to start making personal appearances at nightclubs?"

"When you turn twenty-one," said Donna without missing a beat. "And not a moment sooner."

"Trust me," said Holly, fastening the clasps on the battered guitar case. "I know it sounds exciting, but to be perfectly honest, I'd much rather be back at the hotel, curled up on the bed in my nightie, watching old movies on TV."

"I agree," said Aidan. "I'd much rather be curled up in bed with you, too."

Lark gasped, feeling an overwhelming urge to slap him. But Holly did something even better.

The country star took two slow steps toward Aidan, then leaned in close until her famously full and pouty lips were nearly touching his. "Tell you what, darlin'," she said in a breathy voice. "You can watch old movies with me any time you like ... but if I were you, I'd wait 'til I was old enough to be behind the wheel of a hot little sports car instead of on a li'l ol' bicycle." Winking, she stepped away and added, "So give me a call the minute you get your trainin' wheels off, ya hear?"

Aidan's face turned scarlet as Max, Ollie, and Lark burst into hysterical laughter. Their mocking sounds followed him as he stormed across the patio and into the house.

CHAPTER NINE

"Gone?" Donna's coffee cup stopped midway to her lips. She blinked at Mrs. Fitzpatrick, who had just come in to deliver the news. "What do you mean, 'gone'?"

"I went to wake the boys, like you asked," Mrs. Fitzpatrick explained, her voice disapproving. "Only two of them were in their beds. Aidan is nowhere to be seen. His bed hadn't even been slept in."

"Did you check the music room?" Lark asked. "Maybe he went up there to work on some songs last night and just fell asleep."

"I checked the music room, the pool house, even the garage," Mrs. Fitzpatrick insisted. "The little devil is gone."

It was at this moment that the other two band members came shuffling sleepily into the kitchen.

"Do I smell bangers, Fitzy?" asked Ollie, grinning. "I do love a nice sausage."

"Where is Aidan?" Donna demanded, slamming her coffee mug down.

"Dunno," said Max, yawning. "In the loo, maybe?"

"He's not here," Lark explained. "He's . . . missing."

The boys looked only mildly surprised.

"Do you two know where he is?" cried Donna, her voice growing shrill. "If you do, start talking!"

"We haven't got a clue," Ollie assured her. "Honest."

"Don't you dare cover for him, Oliver," Donna scolded, dragging her hands anxiously through her hair. "That young man is my responsibility. If he's out in a strange city, all alone—" She pulled her frantic eyes from Ollie to glare at Max. "If you know where he went, you'd better tell me right this minute! If he told you what he was planning, or where he was going . . ."

"He didn't tell me anything," said Max. "I'd tell you if he did, I swear."

"Mom," said Lark, struggling to keep calm. "Think about it. Max and Ollie aren't exactly on speaking terms with Aidan right now. What makes you think he'd tell them what he was up to?"

"She's right," said Ollie, then hesitated. "But . . . well, if I had to make an educated guess . . ."

Donna gave him a desperate look. "Go on."

"Aidan's always fancied himself a player. If I had to guess, I'd say he went off to see about catching up with Holly Rose at that club after all."

Donna went pale. "He's fifteen! That's dangerous. And . . . *illegal*!"

Lark picked up her mother's cell phone and began scrolling through her contacts. "I'll call Holly and see if she ran into him." Her finger hovered over the touchscreen. "Or . . . maybe I should call the police?"

"There's always the morgue," said Ollie. "You could try there."

Max elbowed him in the ribs. Lark was about to dial 9-1-1 when a voice floated languidly through the kitchen.

"Morning, all. What's for brekkie?"

All five of them whirled to see a bleary-eyed Aidan lounging in the doorway. He was still dressed in his clothes from the night before—a black leather blazer over a black T-shirt and black leather pants, which made Lark blush as she noticed they fit him like a second skin.

"Either those are some really trendy pajamas, mate," said Ollie, biting back a grin, "or you are well and truly busted."

"Busted?" Aidan gave a casual lift of his eyebrows. "What for? Having a little fun?"

"How about breaking the law?" seethed Donna.

Aidan was cool as a cucumber as he sauntered to the table and helped himself to a glass of juice. "I didn't break any laws. As it happens, I never actually made it *into* the venue."

"Well, if you didn't go to the club, where were you all night?" asked Lark.

"Turns out I wasn't the only one in the queue without proper ID. After I got turned away, I met a couple of girls who couldn't get in, either. They invited me to a party out in the Valley, wherever that is." He gave a careless shrug. "So I went."

"A party in the Valley with two girls you just met." Lark's mother covered her face with her hands and shook her head. "Good grief! Do you have any idea how many things could have gone wrong in that scenario?"

"But nothing did, did it?" Aidan challenged. "I made it home alive, didn't I? Which reminds me, there's a taxi out front and I owe the driver a few dollars for the ride. Donna, would you mind handling that?"

Donna removed her hands from her face and glowered at him.

But Aidan didn't flinch; he simply met her angry eyes with an angelic expression and turned up his palms. "All *my* money's got pictures of Her Majesty the queen on it. Don't think he'd accept that, do you?"

Mrs. Fitzpatrick immediately went to the desk in the corner of the kitchen, where Donna's tote bag hung on the back of a chair. "I'll take care of it," she said, grabbing Donna's wallet and marching out to the driveway.

Aidan just chuckled and took a long sip of his juice.

"Do you think this is funny?" Donna asked in a brittle voice. "Well, here's a little newsflash that you'll find hilarious! What you did last night was not only disrespect-ful and unprofessional, it was downright stupid. And if you ever so much as even *think* about pulling a stunt like that again, I will send you back to London so fast, your head will spin. Do you understand? One more incident and I'm throwing you out of the band."

Lark thought she saw a flash of regret flicker across Aidan's face, but it was almost instantly replaced by a look of defiance. "I thought pop stars were meant to live on the edge! What's the point of being in a band if you can't have any fun?"

"First of all," Donna said tightly, "y'all aren't pop stars yet. You can have your fun when you've earned it. Right now, young man, you have everything to prove. And so far you're doing a pretty terrible job of it!"

It wasn't until Lark heard the "y'all" slip into her mama's speech that she understood just how mad—or maybe frightened—Donna was. From the moment Lark and her mother had arrived in LA, Donna had been obsessed with erasing all traces of Southern twang from her speech. But now she was so angry that she didn't even realize she'd reverted to sounding like a Nashville native again.

Aidan lowered his eyes. But he didn't say he was sorry.

"Get upstairs and change out of that ridiculous outfit," Donna ordered through her teeth. "There were only two art-ists in this whole world who could get away with wearing that much black leather and they were the late, great Johnny Cash and the King of Rock and Roll himself, Elvis Presley." She flung her arm toward the stairs and pointed. "Now, git!"

Git!? Well, that clinched it. Her mother had gone right past anger and straight to fury. If Lark didn't know better, she'd think she was on the verge of sending Aidan out behind the corn crib to cut her a switch to tan his sorry hide!

Okay, maybe that was an exaggeration. But it did do Lark's heart a heap of good to know that somewhere deep down, under all those stylish business suits and designer handbags, her mom still had plenty of Southern sass left in her.

Donna decreed that Aidan stay in his room for the remainder of the day. She never actually said the word "grounded," but her intent was clear. He was under house arrest.

After a tense breakfast, Ollie said he'd like to do a little shopping, so Donna called him a driver and sent him to the mall. Lark knew that her mother would spend most of the day in her office, and Mimi's Sundays were always booked up with church in the morning and family dinner in the late afternoon.

That left her and Max with nothing to do.

She supposed she could make some flimsy excuse about homework and retreat to her bedroom for some much-needed privacy. But as Mrs. Fitzpatrick cleared away the breakfast dishes, she noticed that Max was looking a little gloomy.

"What have you got planned for the day?" Lark asked.

Max shrugged. "Nothing really."

"You didn't want to go shopping with Ollie?"

Max grinned. "I can't afford to buy anything on Rodeo Drive, except maybe a cup of tea. And even that would probably be out of my price range."

Lark laughed. "Well, what do you usually do at home on Sundays?"

"Well, in nice weather, my sister and I take the train to visit our grandparents on the coast. They live in Brighton. It's a fun place, with a beach and a pier." His face lit up as he remembered it, but his smile faded quickly.

"You really are homesick, aren't you?" said Lark.

"Yeah," Max admitted. "I mean, I know what a brilliant opportunity this is, being in LA to pursue a music career. But I really do miss my family. When we're busy with band stuff, I don't feel it much. But when I've got nothing to keep my mind off home, like today, it does sort of get to me. Do you know what I mean?"

Lark nodded. "I know *exactly* what you mean," she said. Then she sprang up from the table. "Don't move. I'll be right back."

She hurried to the pantry, where Mrs. Fitzpatrick was putting away the maple syrup, and whispered her plan to the housekeeper; then she dashed to her mother's office to ask permission. Donna was happy to agree.

Lark bounded back to the kitchen, where Max still sat, looking perplexed.

"I've got an idea that I think will really cheer you up," she said.

"What's that?"

"It's a surprise. Now go get dressed."

Max stared at her for a moment, then stood up. "What should I wear?"

Lark grinned. "Got any swim trunks?"

Max nodded.

"Well, go put them on. We're leaving in ten minutes. Fitzy's going to drive us."

As she watched Max disappear up the stairs, Lark knew there was nothing she could do to cure her own homesickness, but maybe it would help her feel just a little bit better if she could do something to alleviate Max's.

CHAPTER
TEN

"So this is Malibu!" said Max, stretching out his arms and taking in the rolling waves and blazing blue sky. "It's gorgeous."

Lark smiled, but she couldn't quite bring herself to agree . . . not out loud, anyway. Somehow it felt disloyal to acknowledge the sunny splendor of the renowned California beach. Growing up, she'd enjoyed splashing around in the cool, clear lakes of her home state, but if she were being honest, she'd have to admit that even they couldn't compare to the vast, salty waters of the Pacific. She shaded her eyes with her hand and looked toward the horizon, where the sky seemed to melt into the depths of the ocean. There was no denying that it was breathtaking.

"It's nice, I guess," she conceded.

"Wow," said Max, chuckling. "You're a tough one to

impress. Remind me not to ask you what you think of our first single when it comes out."

As Lark had predicted, having sand between his toes was going a long way toward making Max feel better.

They spread a blanket close to the water and feasted on the lunch Mrs. Fitzpatrick had packed at Lark's request.

"Seriously, though," said Max, biting into a roast beef sandwich. "The palm trees, the sunshine, the sound of the surf. Tell the truth . . . some part of you must really love it here on the West Coast."

"You'd think that, wouldn't you?" said Lark with a sigh. "But most of the time, I'm as homesick as you are."

Max reached into the cooler and offered her a pickle, which she took and bit into with a loud crunch. "It's not really about the scenery. Malibu is stunning. Beverly Hills is gorgeous. The weather is perfect. What I miss most about Nashville has nothing to do with any of that. What I miss most is my dad."

"Yeah," said Max. "I've been wondering about what happened between your mum and dad. Donna mentioned she was divorced when we met her in London, but she never elaborated."

"My dad's a session musician, so he travels a lot. And Mom wanted more in the way of a career than she had back in Nashville. Things got tense, and they both became so frustrated that they started arguing about everything from my education to what brand of barbecue sauce to buy. So here we are," she finished sadly. "I suppose I sound like a spoiled brat, whining about living in a huge dang house in one of the most exciting cities in the world."

Max smiled. "A huge 'dang' house, huh?"

"Sorry. My accent gets stronger when I think about home."

"Tell me about your dad, then."

"Right." Lark closed her eyes, picturing him. "Well, he looks like me, I guess. If you can picture me with a couple days' worth of stubble on my chin."

"Nope," said Max. "I can't."

Lark giggled. "He taught me everything I know about music, most of all how to love it. We started writin' songs when I was—"

"Lemme guess . . ." Max said. "Knee-high to a grasshopper?"

"Please!" Lark gave him a pretend haughty look. "I'm a Nashville girl, Max, not some backwater hillbilly. But yes, when I was very small. Dad and I would sit out back and he'd show me how to play chords. I think our first collaboration was a love song to my favorite teddy bear. Do you know how hard it is to find a word to rhyme with 'snuggly'?"

Max laughed. "Um . . . ugly?"

"On weekends Mom would come along and we'd go hiking in the Smoky Mountains. I'd always get tired halfway down, so he'd carry me home on his shoulders."

"He sounds like a perfect dad."

Lark laughed. "Well, he's mostly perfect. Except for when he leaves his stinky hiking boots lying all over the floor, or borrows my guitar pick and forgets to put it back, or when he eats the last piece of fried chicken that I was saving for a midnight treat." But Lark even missed her dad's flaws these days, and would happily put up with his smelly boots.

"Ah."

Lark helped herself to some potato chips, which she washed down with a sip of root beer. Aside from Mimi, she hadn't really talked to anyone about her parents' divorce. It felt good to talk about her dad. Her mom never wanted to talk about the past. She was totally focused on the future. Maybe it was just too painful, Lark suddenly realized.

"Okay, enough about li'l ol' me," she said, turning her accent up to full throttle and batting her eyelashes in an exaggerated Southern Belle gesture. This had Max laughing, which of course was the desired effect. "Let's talk about *you*. How did you, Aidan, and Ollie come to be in a band together? I know you said you met at school, but from the looks of things, y'all can barely stand to be in the same room together, let alone on the same stage."

"We were all at the same school in London," he explained. "I'm a year younger, but Ollie and Aidan had been best friends for most of their childhood. They went to the same private primary school. Me, I'm not from money. But I worked hard and got a scholarship to their private secondary school."

"Good for you," Lark murmured.

"Anyway, Aidan was what you might call a piano prodigy and Ollie can play anything with strings. The music teacher knew I played the drums, so he introduced me to Ollie and we started meeting up after school to practice together. We began writing our own songs and got it in our heads to form a band, so Ollie asked Aidan to join us. We started playing at school assemblies and open mikes all around London, which was how your mum's colleague discovered us. Ollie's dad paid for us to record a demo and we made that silly little video . . . and now here I am, on the beach in Malibu." He polished off his sandwich with a shrug.

So that's what Ollie meant when he said Aidan wouldn't be in the band if it weren't for him. And Aidan repays him by slugging him in the eye! Didn't he know the meaning of the term "loyalty"? Not to mention "friendship"!

Max grinned. "I know what you're thinking. If Ollie and Aidan were so close, then why are they at each other's throats now? Well, there was this girl . . ."

Lark sighed. How many stories about rock bands breaking up began with that exact phrase?

"So Ollie had a girlfriend," Lark ventured, "and Aidan stole her away?"

"Nope. Other way around."

"What?! No!" While Lark could easily imagine Aidan, with his self-important attitude, betraying a friend over a girl, she refused to believe the same of funny, charming Ollie.

"Her name was—is—Jade," Max went on. "Long black hair, hazel eyes, and well fit." He glanced at Lark. "Sorry."

"It's okay. I get it. She's pretty. Keep going."

"She's smart, too. When Aidan met Jade, he was totally into her. Thing was, Jade didn't have the same feelings for Aidan. She went out with him a few times, had a few snogs—"

"Snogs?"

"You know, kisses," Max explained. "But for Jade it was just a casual thing. Nothing more."

"So where does Ollie come in?"

"Not long after we made our video, Jade and her friends came to see us play at a battle of the bands competition in Brighton. Ollie was singing lead vocals, as usual. We were trying out a new song he'd written, a love song. When Jade heard Ollie singin' that love song, she was a goner. Fell for him head over heels."

"Oooh," said Lark. "That's not good."

"She dumped Aidan straightaway, wouldn't take his calls or even acknowledge him at school. I'm not Aidan Harrington's biggest fan, but even I felt bad for the guy. He was crushed."

"And Ollie started going out with Jade."

Max shook his head. "No. I think he fancied her, but he kept his distance. For Aidan's sake."

"He's a good friend."

"Aidan didn't see it that way. Things between Ollie and Aidan haven't been the same since. The band would have probably split up, but when Donna offered us a deal, we decided to stick together."

"That's terrible."

They were quiet for a moment, enjoying the sound of the crashing surf and the squeals of swooping seagulls. Lark snuck a glance at Max and saw that he was still thinking about his friends. Clearly, being caught in the middle was making him miserable. She decided to change the subject.

"Did you always want to be a rock star, Max?"

"Sure. But to be honest, I would have rather waited a bit. You know, finish school, be a kid for a while."

Lark gave him a confused look. "So why did you agree to sign with my mom's label and come to LA?"

"Because," said Max, squirming uneasily. "My family could really use the money. Dad and Mum work real hard, but they're always behind with bills. If I can make it in the music world, I'll be able to help them out."

Lark nodded, understanding perfectly. For Max, just like for Donna and Lark, there was a lot riding on the success of Abbey Road.

"How about a swim?" Max suggested.

Lark didn't have to be asked twice. She was on her feet and dashing toward the surf even before Max had put down his bottle of root beer. It never occurred to her to feel self-conscious about being in a bathing suit, either. Max was starting to feel like the big brother she'd never had.

As Lark and Max dove into the crystal-clear ocean, they sang the Beatles' "Here Comes the Sun" at the top of their lungs. It almost seemed as if the classic song had been written for this very moment, as the warm ocean water and California sunshine helped dissolve the sadness in their hearts.

CHAPTER ELEVEN

Lark woke up on Monday morning feeling relaxed and with just the tiniest sunburn across the bridge of her nose. Checking her reflection in the mirror, she smiled. The extra color made her green eyes "pop," as the beauty magazines would say. She wondered if Teddy Reese would notice when they met after school to rehearse.

She hurried down to the kitchen, where she found her mother in a terrible mood.

"Now what?" asked Lark, not really wanting to know the answer. Today was going to be a great day and she didn't want anything to mess it up. She couldn't wait to get to school. It was the day of the school's International Fair. There were tables set up all around the gym with parents and grandparents offering foods and displaying examples of their cultures of origin. Since most kids in LA thought of the Deep South as practically a foreign country, Lark had considered asking her mom to whip up a batch of homemade biscuits and Southern fried chicken. But Donna hadn't fried anything since they'd arrived in California. Lark suspected this was only partly due to the new image her mother was cultivating; the other reason was that a person probably couldn't even *find* chicken with the skin still on it anywhere within the city limits of Los Angeles . . . let alone a tub of Crisco!

"Some music blogger was at that club where Holly appeared on Saturday night," Donna reported. "He wrote a great piece about Holly, but he also recognized Aidan from the footage of Holly that Mimi posted online. There's a whole paragraph about a member of a band called Abbey Road acting obnoxious and trying to get into the club."

Lark stuffed a water bottle into her backpack. "Oh, no."

"'Oh, no' is an understatement. The boys are supposed to be behaving themselves. That's the marketing angle I'm aiming for. Wholesome. Clean-cut. I want them to be the sort of boys a mother wouldn't be afraid to let her daughter date."

"They're normal teenagers, Mom. They have personalities, not PR agendas. Aidan just made a mistake." She was surprised to hear herself sticking up for Aidan, but Max's story about Jade had caused her to see the group's "bad boy" in a different light. He had feelings, just like anyone else. His broken heart didn't excuse his actions or make him any less of a jerk for sneaking out, but she couldn't help defending him. "Besides, what are the chances anyone's going to read that blog anyway?"

"High, given that it includes a link to Mimi's footage of Holly Rose. I need to do some damage limitation to improve their image. But that'll take time. And I didn't budget for it."

"Well, how about you dress them in white robes and angel wings and let them hand out signed photos of themselves on the corner of Hollywood and Vine?" She knew her tone was snippy, but what difference did it make? Her mother never listened to her anyway. "Maybe you can send them off to plant trees in the rain forest, or figure out a way for them to single-handedly save the whales?" Lark picked up her backpack and headed for the foyer. "Oh, I've got it!" she called over her shoulder sarcastically. "Since today is my school's International Fair day, you can have them play a free concert to benefit the youth of America."

"What did you say?" came her mother's voice from the kitchen.

"Nothing, Mom. Nothing at all," said Lark. Then she headed out the door before Donna could say another word.

At school, Lark saw the opportunity for a little fun from halfway down the hall. Mimi was standing at her open locker, focused on something inside as if she were in a trance. Lark tiptoed until she was mere inches away, then poked her head around Mimi's locker door, and shouted, "Boo!"

Mimi jumped and let out a little yelp, dropping her history textbook and quickly closing her locker door. "Lark! O-M-G! Way to sneak up on a person and give her a heart attack!" But she was smiling. And maybe even blushing.

"Sorry," said Lark, laughing. "But you were totally zoned out. What are you doing so intently?"

"Um . . . you know . . . just redecorating."

This was odd. Lark knew that lots of kids bedecked the interior of their lockers with small posters, magazine cut-outs, or bumper stickers. She would bet her boots that Alessandra Drake had a photo of Teddy Reese in hers. And a mirror, of course. Lark herself had an old family photo pinned to the inside of her locker door with a magnet in the shape of a treble clef. But Mimi was a minimalist. She liked to keep her locker neat and streamlined, so as not to clutter her mind and prevent creative thinking.

"Decorating, hmm?" Lark grinned. "Can I see?"

Mimi sighed and rolled her eyes. "Okay . . . go ahead."

Lark opened the locker and wasn't surprised to see that Mimi had printed out one of the pictures of Ollie she'd taken over the weekend. It was a great shot of him holding his guitar. "I had a feeling," she said, giggling. "It's an awesome photo."

Mimi smiled. "Well, it would be hard to take a *bad* picture of Oliver. He's gorgeous. But it's more than just his looks. He's so funny. And so talented! And that accent is adorable. He's, like, the perfect guy."

Lark gave her friend a serious look. "You know he's fifteen, right?" she said gently. "I mean, it's okay to have a crush and all, but he's a lot older than you are."

"Oh, I know," said Mimi lightly. "But it's fun to . . . ya know . . . daydream."

Lark certainly couldn't argue with that. She'd been daydreaming about Teddy Reese since the day she first laid eyes on him.

"How's Oliver's cheek?" Mimi asked. "Is there a mark? And Aidan's nose? Is it still swollen?"

As the girls made their way toward their first-period classes, Lark filled her friend in on Aidan's latest escapade. Mimi was appalled, although pleased to hear that a blogger was sharing her footage of the band.

"That could have been a disaster," she said as they reached the junction of the science hall and the foreign language corridor. This was where they parted ways every morning, Mimi heading off to French class and Lark to chem lab. Ordinarily, they'd meet up again at lunch, but today the whole school would enjoy an abbreviated schedule to accommodate the International Fair festivities.

"Meet me at the origami booth," Mimi said, dashing off down the hall. "Trevor Yoshida promised me his grandma would teach me how to make a tiny movie camera out of folded paper."

"I think he might be pulling your leg!" Lark called after her. "But okay!"

The first three classes of the day were basically useless. Everyone was either excited to get to the caf-a-gym-a-torium to sample the tacos and eggrolls and baklava, or else they were worrying about the presentations they had to deliver *about* those tacos and eggrolls and baklava. Emma DiGiorgio, Lark's lab partner, was slated to give a talk about how to make the perfect antipasto, and the thought of it had her so distracted, she nearly burned off the end of her ponytail with the Bunsen burner. "What if I mispronounce 'prosciutto'?" she whispered to Lark. "What if I forget to mention that the anchovies are optional? *Always* optional!"

Finally, it was time for the International Fair to begin. As Lark filed into the space with the rest of her classmates, she caught an image of Alessandra Drake . . . wearing a tiara!

"What's that about?" she whispered to Emma.

"Alessandra claims she can trace her ancestry all the way back to fourteenth-century British nobility."

Lark frowned. "Does that make her a royal?"

"Yeah," said Emma with a grin. "A royal pain in the butt."

"Hey, Lark!" came Mimi's voice from across the room.

Lark wished Emma luck on her presentation, and headed through the crowd to where Mimi was waiting at the Japanese origami exhibit.

"Wow," said Lark, taking in the magical sight of miniature paper cranes and swans. "These are amazing!"

"Turns out there's no such thing as an origami camera after all," Mimi huffed. "You were right. Trevor was just joking with me."

Lark smiled. "Maybe he just wanted to be sure you stopped by his booth. Maybe he likes you."

"Ya think?" Mimi beamed. "Well, he's no Oliver Wesley, but he *is* kinda cute." She picked up two squares of paper and handed one to Lark. "Let's give it a shot."

Taking their cue from Baba Yoshida, the girls carefully folded the sheets of colored paper into delicate angular designs. Mimi, ever the creative one, produced a perfect pink horse, but Lark's neon-green bunny rabbit was hopelessly lopsided.

Their next stop was Emma's booth, where they sampled delicious little cannolis from her nonno's Italian bakery. Then they enjoyed a brief demonstration of Indian dance, performed by Alia Chopra and her two older sisters.

"Her costume is beautiful," Lark whispered, admiring Alia's jangly bangles and wristlets, and her shimmering satin pants embroidered with golden thread.

"She's so graceful," Mimi noted. "And their dresses look amazing when they spin around."

Lark knew her friend well enough to know that Mimi was already planning to ask Alia if she could film her doing one of these traditional dances.

When the dance performance was over, Lark and Mimi moved on, following their noses toward the most delicious aroma in the whole gym.

Gingerbread!

"Whose stall is this?" Mimi wondered aloud, sidling up to the table that held platters piled high with gingerbread cookies. Some were cut in the shapes of little boys and girls, others were heart-shaped, but all of them looked equally yummy.

Someone's grandma, a pretty, white-haired woman in glasses, sat primly behind the gingerbread table, offering tubes of squeezable icing to her many eager cookie samplers.

"Do we really have to waste time decorating them?" Mimi joked. "Can't we just go straight to eating them?"

"It'll be fun," said Lark, accepting a tube of pink icing and choosing a large, heart-shaped cookie.

Mimi chose a gingerbread man and got busy icing his head with a sugary mass of yellow hair. Next, she dotted the face with two blue eyes.

Lark giggled. "Did you seriously just decorate that cookie to look like Ollie?"

Mimi nodded. "Not that I had to. The real Oliver is sweet enough."

Lark positioned her icing tube over her cookie. She willed herself not to inscribe it with the initials "L.C." and "T.R." Instead, she wrote her name in pink loopy script. Then she nibbled off the pointy bottom and let out a sigh of absolute delight.

"How's it taste?" asked Mimi, unable to bring herself to chomp into cookie-Ollie's head.

"It tastes . . . ," said Lark, letting the spicy sweetness fill her mouth, "like a Christmas carol."

"What a wonderful compliment," the grandma said. "I've never had my baking compared to music before." She peered through her glasses at the pink writing on Lark's cookie.

"Lark?" she read. "Are you Lark Campbell?"

The question took Lark by surprise. She'd never met this woman before, so there was no reason for her to know Lark's last name. But she answered with a polite, "Yes, ma'am," before taking another bite of her cookie.

"Oh!" cried the woman, reaching out her dainty hand to shake. "I've heard so much about you from my grandson."

Lark wanted to ask who her grandson was, but her mouth was filled with cookie. She didn't have to wonder long, because in the next moment, a voice behind her was saying, "Hey, Gran. Looks like your cookies are going down well."

Lark turned to see Teddy Reese approaching the ginger-bread booth. He leaned down to kiss his grandma on the cheek. Then he turned back to Lark, who was discreetly attempting to brush the cookie crumbs from her lips and chin.

"Eat up," he advised with a grin. "You need plenty of energy for our rehearsal this afternoon."

Lark desperately wanted to offer a cute response, but if she attempted to gulp down her enormous mouthful of cookie, she'd probably choke to death. Fortunately, she was saved from having to speak by the squeal of feedback over the caf-a-gym-a-torium's loudspeaker.

"May I have your attention, please," boomed Principal Hardy's cheerful voice. "Boys and girls, family and friends, attention, please."

It was a moment before the din died down. Lark took the opportunity to swallow hard and offer Teddy a shy smile. Then she turned to the stage at the far end of the room, where the principal stood holding a portable microphone. Behind Principal Hardy, the stage curtain opened and Lark saw that there were three mike stands, an electronic keyboard, and a drum kit.

A feeling of dread shot through her. *Oh, no. OH, NO . . .*

"In addition to all the wonderful food and fascinating cultural exhibits you've been enjoying," the principal announced, "we have a big surprise for you. Thanks to one of our students, today, for the first time ever on American soil, a brand-new British rock band is going to perform their as-yet-unreleased new song. Isn't it fitting that on this day when we celebrate different nations around the globe, we get to enjoy a true *world* premiere!"

128

Immediately, murmurs filled the gym. Kids were whispering, making guesses as to who might be performing. And, of course, wondering which of their classmates had been cool enough to bring in a rock band for the International Fair.

Lark, of course, didn't have to wonder. Because she knew.

To her horror, the principal stepped aside and suddenly Donna Campbell was at one of the microphones. Lark's stomach flipped over, threatening to bring up her gingerbread cookie. *No! No, no, no. Mama, why?*

"Are you okay?" Teddy asked.

"Not really," Lark replied.

"Hello, everyone," said Donna, beaming around at the curious crowd. "I'm Lark Campbell's mother."

CHAPTER TWELVE

Hundreds of pairs of eyes began to search the room. Lark heard a few students asking, "Who's Lark Campbell?" while others whispered, "Never heard of her," which made Lark want to crawl under the gingerbread table and hide.

"I am very happy to present," Lark's mother continued brightly, "all the way from London, the hottest new British export . . . Abbey Road!" She turned to the wings and waved the boys onto the stage. Aidan slunk to the keyboard, looking moody. Max seemed friendly and focused as he took his place at the drum set. And Ollie, ever the front man, was working the crowd—waving and smiling before he'd played a single note on his guitar.

The mood in the caf-a-gym-a-torium shifted from mildly interested to full-on anticipation. Girls were gasping and giggling, boys were hollering and clapping. Everything about the three Brits on stage said "cool," and it didn't hurt that they were gorgeous.

"Hello, Ronald Reagan Middle School!"

A cheer went up as what seemed like the entire student body rushed the stage. Lark saw Ollie throw Max a grin; they were totally in their element!

"We're Abbey Road," Ollie said, "and it's awesome to be here! We're going to play our soon-to-be-released new single 'Dream of Me,' and we really hope you like it!"

There were more shouts and applause as Ollie counted his bandmates in. The infectious intro had everyone bouncing, and eight counts later, Ollie's voice filled the gym.

"*Do you dream of me when the nights are long? When the world is dark, do you hear this song . . .*"

Mimi, who had probably listened to "Dream of Me" a zillion times since Saturday, was singing along at the top of her lungs. She knew every word by heart. Lark did, too, but she wasn't exactly in a sing-along mood.

Suddenly, Alessandra Drake was at Lark's side. "You *know* them?" she demanded.

"Um . . . well . . ." Lark had to blink against the glare of Lady Drake's tiara.

"Oh, she doesn't just *know* them," Mimi interjected smugly. "She *lives* with them."

"You *live* with them?" Alessandra said incredulously.

"You live with *them*?" Teddy repeated.

But whereas Alessandra's tone had been one of complete and utter disbelief, Teddy hadn't sounded as if he doubted it at all. If anything he sounded a little . . . *jealous*, as if he didn't particularly like the thought of these three guys being around Lark twenty-four/seven. This sent a shiver up her spine, and for a moment Lark forgot her anger at Donna for springing this very unwelcome surprise on her.

"Lark's mother is their manager," Mimi explained. "So they're living in Lark's house, which means she gets to eat all her meals with them and even rehearse with them. And I'm sort of the unofficial in-house videographer, so I do, too. And they even asked us to be their backup dancers." The unspoken *Take that, Alessandra* seemed to sizzle in the air.

The song had reached the chorus, and kids were singing along. When "Dream of Me" ended, the whole gym erupted into raucous applause. All except Teddy and Lark, who clapped politely.

And then, Alessandra Drake—tiara and all—turned to Lark with the broadest, chummiest smile Lark had ever seen.

"O-M-G," she gushed, placing her hand on Lark's arm as if they'd been best friends since birth. "You totally should invite me over to your house so I can meet them."

Mimi let out a snort. "Fat chance," she grumbled, but in the tumult of cheering and screaming, the comment went unheard. In the next second, Alessandra had dashed off to join the starstruck mob.

"Was it my imagination," said Mimi dryly, "or was she actually drooling?"

But Lark wasn't in the mood for jokes. Her stomach had begun to roil again as her mother returned to the stage. *What next? A PowerPoint presentation of my baby pictures?*

"So, what do you think, kids?" her mother asked. "Have we got a hit on our hands?"

The crowd roared, then roared even louder when Max made a dazzling show of twirling his drumsticks. He looked like some old-time western gunslinger spinning his pistols before a shoot-out. Lark's mom allowed the thunderous ovation to go on for another full minute, then motioned for the crowd to settle down.

"Does anyone have any questions for the boys?" she asked.

Hands shot up all over the room.

"What are your names?" a girl shouted. "Starting with the cute one."

As if on cue, all three boys spoke their names in unison, inciting more laughter.

"How long are you staying in LA?" asked another girl.

"As long as you'll have us," replied Max with a grin.

This response was met with shrieks and giggles. Lark thought she saw Emma DiGiorgio's knees buckle.

Now Principal Hardy returned to the stage with a slight frown. "Remember, boys and girls, this is the International Fair, so your questions are supposed to be about life in England. The culture, the politics, the lifestyle, the people . . ."

Alessandra's hand shot up. "I have a question about the people."

"Yes, Alessandra?" the principal prompted.

"Are all the people in England as gorgeous and talented as you three?"

Another stern look from Principal Hardy steered the interview in the appropriate direction. The boys were asked about English food, whether they liked soccer, and whether or not London Bridge really was, in fact, falling down.

Then, after Abbey Road performed "Promises to Keep," Principal Hardy thanked them for their surprise appearance and the boys left the stage to more screaming and cheering. Lark's mom couldn't have looked happier.

For Lark, on the other hand, it was going to be a very long day.

When the International Fair ended, Lark's mother was waiting for her by the gym doors.

"Wasn't that wonderful?" Donna gushed. "Your friends loved them, and performing for the school will really help the boys' wholesome image."

"My *friends*?" hissed Lark. "I've never even spoken to half these people, but suddenly, everyone is coming up to me, asking me for my phone number and wondering if we can hang out sometime."

"Even better," said Donna. "I got some free focus testing, and you're meeting new people."

"People who never gave me a second look before, but now want to use me to meet pop stars," Lark spat.

Donna looked genuinely confused and Lark realized with a jolt that she hadn't exactly been forthcoming with her mother regarding her social standing at school.

"Forget it," Lark muttered. "I just wish you'd asked me if I was okay with this stupid concert-slash-focus group."

The joy in her mother's face had vanished. "I'm sorry, honey. You were the one who gave me the idea. I thought you'd be pleased. I honestly never meant to make you uncomfortable." She made a tenuous attempt at a smile. "How about I sign you out early and you and I and the boys can go for a late lunch?"

"No, thank you," said Lark, her voice cold. "I can't miss an entire afternoon of classes. In fact, I'll be home later than usual today because I'm meeting someone after school to—" She was about to say rehearse but thought better of it. "To study," she said. "And if you're wondering, it has nothing to do with your surprise performance. It was arranged last week."

"Lark—"

But Lark wasn't finished yet. "You know what's funny?" she barreled on. "The whole time we've been here, you've been too busy to take part in my school stuff. You've never once showed your face in this building! Not for a parent-teacher meeting, not for the wrapping paper fund-raiser, not even when I got that stupid ribbon in my English class for winning the poetry contest! But the minute there was a chance for you to do something in *your* interest, you just couldn't get here fast enough!"

Donna sighed. "I wish you could understand that I'm doing all of this for us, Lark. For our future."

Deep down, Lark did understand, but that didn't stop her from rolling her eyes and storming off down the hall.

For the rest of the day, she was ambushed by kids desperate for information about Abbey Road. Her seventh-grade classmates asked for autographed pictures and free music downloads. The eighth graders were bolder; they wanted to know if she could get them concert tickets complete with backstage passes. One girl actually invited herself to sleep over at Lark's house! Lark intended to say no, but she was so shocked that she couldn't even formulate a reply. For all she knew, the eighth grader was going to show up on their doorstep that very night, holding a sleeping bag and expecting a slumber party!

When the last class bell blared, Lark thought she might actually cry with relief.

And then she remembered . . . she was meeting Teddy! Things suddenly seemed a whole lot brighter.

CHAPTER
THIRTEEN

Lark had to force herself not to run all the way to the music room. When she arrived, she was thrilled to see through the narrow window in the door that Teddy was already there, as though he, too, couldn't wait to start working together. As she quietly pushed the door open, she heard piano music and Teddy's voice filling the space.

Now who was in danger of swooning?

His eyes were closed and he was singing a ballad that Lark didn't recognize. The lyrics were sad and yet hopeful at the same time.

When he finished, she stepped into the practice room. "That was incredible."

Teddy looked up from the piano keys, startled.

"Oh, hey," he said, slightly flustered. "I was just warming up."

"Didn't mean to startle you," Lark apologized, closing the door behind her. "But really, that sounded amazing."

"Thanks. It's one of the songs I'm considering for the talent show." He paused, then added, "I wrote it myself."

Lark couldn't believe what he'd just said. "So you don't just sing; you write and play the piano, too?"

"Been taking lessons since I was five," said Teddy, playing a few ominous chords.

Lark gave him a quizzical look. "Not to sound ungrateful for the invitation, but what do you need me for?"

"Because," said Teddy, the corner of his mouth quirking up into a half grin. "In the world of middle-school talent shows, guitar is much cooler than piano."

Lark wasn't sure she agreed. Plenty of cool musicians—country and rock 'n' roll alike—played the piano. But she wasn't about to talk herself out of an afternoon in Teddy's company. So she crossed the room and took the best available acoustic guitar off its stand. Then she fished a pick out of the old, chipped coffee mug Mr. Saunders kept on top of the upright piano. The mug was emblazoned with the words, If Music Be the Food of Love . . . Let's Eat!

"I think your song is great. What's it called?"

"'Midnight,'" he replied. "And it's not great. Not yet, anyway. But if your songwriting is as good as Mr. Saunders says it is, I was hoping you could help me get it there."

"Sure," said Lark. "I'd love to."

Teddy gave her an appreciative smile that had her gripping the neck of the guitar. If the instrument were human, she'd be strangling it.

He reached for the sheet music. "I've only got the one copy, but—"

"That's okay," said Lark. Perching herself on a stool across from Teddy, Lark positioned the guitar over her thighs. "Gimme a sec," she said, arranging her fingers on the frets.

Just as Teddy had done, she closed her eyes and began to play the song she'd just heard him perform. Most people called this "playing by ear," but Lark never liked that description. For her, music used more than just her sense of hearing. Lark actually visualized the music. She called it "hearing with her eyes" and it came as naturally to her as breathing. For a long time she believed all musicians perceived music in shapes, colors, and textures as well as sounds, but when she asked her father about it, he promised her that this was something unique. Lark had tried to describe it to Mimi once, explaining that it was as if all her senses came together to become a brand-new sense that allowed her to experience a song with every atom of her being. Sometimes she'd even swear she could smell and taste it.

Mimi, an artist herself, had found this fascinating. Lark was just relieved her friend hadn't alerted the nearest mental institution to come with a straitjacket and lock her away.

She let her fingers take over, translating the musical vision from her mind to the guitar. "Okay, so . . . D, and then G, and then E minor . . ." She strummed and heard the rich fullness of the chords and knew she was dead on.

"Unbelievable," said Teddy, shaking his head in awe. "You got it. Just like that."

Lark felt her cheeks turn pink. "Well, it was pretty easy, it's very repetitive. Not in a bad way—it's catchy."

She took a few minutes to practice and when she was comfortable with the whole song, they tried it together.

From the minute her fingers touched the strings and Teddy's voice broke into song, magic happened. The music and lyrics seemed to intertwine and become something else, something singular and new and entirely theirs.

When Teddy came to the refrain, something in his expression changed. His eyes widened in surprise and he looked very pleased. Lark smiled back at him and kept playing.

Before she knew it, Teddy was singing the last lyric and as he held the note, it seemed to tremble in the air. Lark thought there was something peculiar about the timbre of it, as if there were some sort of echo.

"You were perfect," she said.

"Thanks. So were you. Really." Teddy reached for two bottles of water on the windowsill and handed one to Lark. "But I thought you said you didn't want to sing."

Lark blinked, confused. "I don't."

"Hmm . . ." Teddy smiled. "Well, you did."

"*What?*" Lark nearly choked on her water. "I did not."

"Yes, you did. Well, not all of it. Just the chorus. It sounded incredible. We harmonized."

"We did?" Lark was flat-out astounded. That explained why he'd looked so surprised when he first sang the chorus and why the last word of the song had that depth she'd thought she'd only imagined. She'd been singing!

Not just in front of Teddy Reese. *With* Teddy Reese.

"Please let me talk you into doing that for the talent show," he said, screwing the plastic cap back onto his water bottle. "Even if you only want to sing the chorus, that would be amazing."

Lark opened her mouth to say no, but his eyes were so hopeful and his smile was so sweet. He could probably have asked her to smash that guitar over her own head right that very minute and she'd have had a hard time refusing. When she didn't answer, he shrugged.

"Just think about it," he said. "I don't want to pressure you. But seriously . . . we sounded great. It was like . . ."

"Magic." The word was out before Lark could stop herself. Again, she felt her face flushing.

"Yeah," said Teddy. "Exactly. Magic."

It was quiet for a moment. Lark's heart was pounding so hard, she wondered if he could hear it. "Okay, I'll think about it," she said at last, her voice barely a whisper.

"You're the best," said Teddy.

They spent the next several minutes tweaking the song. At first, Lark was hesitant to criticize Teddy's work, but he assured her he wanted her input. So she made a few small suggestions for changes to the melody and chorus, which Teddy enthusiastically accepted. Then she helped him improve the lyrics a bit. It felt as if they'd been writing songs together forever.

"Well," said Teddy, with a reluctant glance at the clock. "I guess we'd better get going. My mom's probably waiting outside school."

But for some reason, he didn't move an inch.

"Me too," said Lark at last. But she didn't make any attempt to leave, either.

There was a knock on the door and Mr. Saunders poked his head in. "How are things going?"

"Great," said Teddy. "We had an awesome rehearsal."

"Something told me you would," said the music teacher with a wink. "I really hate to rush you two, but I've got an oboe lesson scheduled in five minutes."

"We're all done for today," said Teddy, reaching for his backpack. "Can we use the space again tomorrow?"

"Certainly," said Mr. Saunders, settling himself on the piano bench. "See you then."

It was a minute before Lark realized this was her cue to exit. Teddy was already at the door. Was he actually waiting for her? That would be too much to hope for. And if he was, the thought of making conversation from the music wing all the way to the driveway where the late bus would be waiting was simply too terrifying to even consider.

"I'll see you tomorrow," she said, sliding off the stool and taking her time crossing the room to the guitar stands.

"Oh. Okay." Teddy sounded a little disappointed as he opened the door. "Well, see ya tomorrow." A second later he was gone.

"Don't you need to catch the late bus, Miss Campbell?" Mr. Saunders asked, checking his watch.

"Yes, sir," Lark said, picking up her backpack. With a wave to her music teacher, Lark sprinted off to catch her bus.

Lark hurried into the house. She couldn't wait to Skype Mimi and tell her all about rehearsing with Teddy.

She was halfway up the stairs when she heard piano music coming from the living room.

The melody was terrific. And familiar. In fact, it was *very* familiar.

Lark spun on her heel, flew down the steps, and stomped into the living room, just in time to hear her mother gushing with delight.

"Aidan, it's wonderful!" Donna cried. "You've completely nailed it. This is the new song we've been waiting for. I think we can definitely make this one of the tracks on Abbey Road's first album."

"What's going on?" Lark demanded, her eyes shooting across the room to lock on Aidan's.

"Lark," said her mother, "Aidan was just playing me 'Missing You.' It's his new song."

"Was he?" Lark seethed. "And how exactly is he defining it as 'his'?"

"As in he wrote the song himself, of course." Donna beamed at Aidan, who was seated at the piano. "Go ahead," she said. "Play your song for Lark."

Without even flinching, Aidan swiveled around and played the song—"Homesick"—he'd stolen from Lark's songwriting journal.

He'd made a few subtle changes here and there, to create a pop-ier sound, but there was no doubt that Aidan was performing her song and claiming it as his own!

Lark's head was spinning. How dare he? Along with her fury came a crushing sense of mortification, as she realized that "Homesick" wasn't the only thing he would have found in her journal. All her secret poems about Teddy were written down in there, along with her silly little "Lark and Teddy" doodles.

When he finished playing, Aidan turned to Lark. His expression was infuriatingly composed. His dark eyes gleamed, almost as if he were challenging her to say something.

Did he really think she *wouldn't*? Was he so arrogant that he actually thought he could get away with this?

She swallowed hard, struggling to find her voice, her whole body shaking with anger. It was as if Aidan had stolen away not only the words to her song, but every other word she'd ever known as well. Because suddenly, she couldn't manage to formulate a single sound, let alone an accusation. She simply stood there, overwhelmed with fury and completely mute.

"I know!" her mom said, mistaking Lark's silence for awe. "It leaves you speechless, doesn't it? Since Aidan and Ollie couldn't seem to agree on anything, I was beginning to worry that we wouldn't have enough material for an album. But it seems Aidan works better on his own. He's saved the day with this gem of a song!"

"Must be all the lovely sunshine that's inspired me," Aidan said, his voice dripping with false modesty.

"I told you it would come," Lark's mom gushed. "All writers get writer's block from time to time."

"One minute there was nothing, and the next, I had a whole song."

There's a word for that, Lark thought bitterly. *It's "plagiarism."*

All she had to do was say it. All she had to do was tell her mother the truth and Aidan Harrington would be on the next plane back to London.

And that, of course, was the problem. The realization hit Lark like a punch. Aidan had already been warned about his reckless conduct; there was no way her mother would tolerate another instance of bad behavior. And ripping off the manager's daughter certainly qualified. If her mom knew Aidan had stolen Lark's work, surely she'd send him packing and that would be the end of Abbey Road. All the time and money she'd already invested would have been wasted. Any possibility of Lotus Records' turning a profit would be destroyed. She wasn't ready to do that to her mother.

"Lark, where are your manners?" her mother prompted, laughing. "Tell Aidan what you think of his song." Then she headed out of the room, shouting over her shoulder, "I'm just going to call the office and tell them the good news—we have a future hit on our hands!"

Lark clenched her fists and took a deep breath. "I love the song," she said through gritted teeth. "In fact, I couldn't love it more if I had written it myself."

Aidan replied with a triumphant smirk.

The subtle route clearly wasn't going to work. "You stole my song," she accused him.

"Prove it," Aidan challenged her. "Go get your little diary and show your mummy. I'm sure she'd be *very* interested to read all about your crush."

Lark's cheeks burned with embarrassment and indignation. She felt sick at the thought of Aidan laughing at her lovesick doodles—and even sicker at the thought of showing them to her mom.

"I did us all a favor," Aidan hissed. "We need a hit—your mom more than anyone. So what if I got a little, er, *inspiration* from your notebook. If you rat on me, we don't have a song. And if we don't have a song, we don't have an album, so you can kiss this fancy house good-bye."

Lark stared at Aidan, speechless at his audacity. Then she bolted from the room before he could see her tears. She knew what this could mean for Lotus Records—and for her mom—but she had to do what was right. She couldn't let Aidan get away with this.

CHAPTER FOURTEEN

"He is *such* a jerk!" said Mimi. Her face on Lark's computer screen looked angry and concerned. "Why didn't you tell your mom he was lying?"

Lark drew a deep, shuddering breath and wiped her wet cheeks with the back of her hand. She'd already been crying for half an hour when the distinctive Skype chimes had alerted her to Mimi's call. She'd answered with a fresh burst of sobs that had Mimi fearing the worst—that things with Teddy had been a disaster.

But a tearful Lark had informed Mimi that the first Reese-Campbell collaboration had been nothing short of perfection. It was the rest of the afternoon that had totally sucked. Then, with her stomach churning and her heart aching, she'd told Mimi about Aidan ripping off her new song.

"You can't let that thieving creep do this, Lark," Mimi advised. "You have to tell your mother the truth!"

"I know, but what difference would it make? Aidan would just say I was the one who was lying and make me prove I wrote the song."

"Which you can do easily enough by showing your mother your songwriting journal."

"You know I can't do that," said Lark with a quiver in her voice. "I'd die of embarrassment. She'll tell me I'm too young to be thinking about boys. Then she'll take all my songs, add a techno backbeat, and sell them to some ditzy blond pop-star wannabe for zillions of dollars."

"I seriously doubt that," said Mimi, rolling her eyes. "But just out of curiosity, which scares you more? Your mom knowing you like Teddy, or your mom knowing you write awesome songs?"

"The Teddy thing, I guess," Lark confessed. "I mean, *maybe* I could bring myself to prove Aidan stole my song if there was a way to do it without handing over my private journal. But it's too humiliating. I mean, c'mon. I bet you didn't tell your mom you have a giant crush on Ollie."

"I didn't have to," said Mimi. "The eight million pictures I now have hanging all over my room sort of gave it away."

Lark giggled despite her horrible mood and considered her options. "I suppose my mom wouldn't exactly be shocked to find out about my songwriting. I *am* my dad's daughter, after all. She probably suspects I've got a song or two in me."

"A song or *two*? Girlfriend, you are a bottomless pit of music and lyrics!" Mimi laughed, then tilted her head thoughtfully. "Could it be that it's not the thought of some ditzy blonde singing your songs that scares you? Maybe what really terrifies you is knowing that if your mom did find out how much talent you've got, she'd be doing the same thing to you that she's doing to Abbey Road. She'd be doing everything in her power to make *you* a star."

Lark bit her lip. "Maybe. I guess."

"For most singers, that would be a dream come true."

"Yeah, well, for me, it's my worst nightmare."

Mimi was quiet for a moment. "Lark," she said at last, "did you ever think that maybe this is all happening for a reason? I know Aidan did a crummy thing, but won't you even entertain the possibility that this is just the universe's way of telling you it's time to let the whole world know what a super-gifted singer-songwriter you are?" Mimi shrugged. "I'm just sayin' . . . it might be time for you to face this crazy stage fright of yours and sing in front of people."

"I'm playing guitar in the talent show," Lark said, hating the whine in her voice. "Isn't that enough?"

"Yeah, about that . . ." On the computer screen, Mimi's expression showed a flicker of hurt.

"What's wrong?" asked Lark.

"Well, it's just that, when I asked you if I could premiere our music video as part of the talent show, you flat-out refused because you didn't want to be on display. But when Teddy came along and batted his big blue eyes at you, you jumped at the chance."

Lark frowned. "He didn't bat. And I didn't jump. It was just . . . I don't know . . . different."

"Right," Mimi grumbled. "Different." She sighed and shook her head. "I gotta go," she said curtly. "Homework."

"Meems, wait . . ."

But Mimi was gone.

"Could this day get any worse?" Lark asked out loud. "I mean, really. What else has the universe got planned for me today?"

It was at that moment, as if the so-called universe had decided to answer her, that Lark's phone dinged, alerting her to a new message.

It was from Mimi. So maybe her best friend wasn't as angry as she'd seemed.

With a surge of hope, Lark opened the message, then frowned in confusion at the YouTube link Mimi had sent her. "A video?"

She looked at the message Mimi had included: SHOW THIS TO YOUR MOM. I'LL TAKE IT DOWN AS SOON AS YOU DO. Lark smiled as realization dawned. "A *video*!"

Lark sprang off the bed, ran down the hall, and flew down the stairs.

She burst into her mother's office with one word on her lips. "'Homesick'!" she cried, holding out her smartphone.

Donna looked up from a pile of paperwork at her desk. "Still? Well, I'm sorry honey, I know you miss Nashville, but this is where we live now."

"No!" said Lark. "I'm not telling you that I *am* homesick . . . I mean, I *am*, but that's not the point. I want you to see a video. Of a song called 'Homesick.'"

She thrust the phone under her mother's nose.

"What's this?" Donna smiled in anticipation. "A new act you want me to see?"

"*God* no!" Lark ground her teeth in frustration. "It is definitely not a new 'act.' Heck, is that all you ever think about? Business? For once, can something *not* be about an act or a deal or a brand marketing strategy?"

"Lark, *what* are you talking about?"

"I'm talking about *this*," Lark hollered, shaking the phone. "I'm talking about me!"

Hand trembling, she hit the Play arrow and handed the phone to her mom. The tiny screen came alive with an image of Lark strumming her guitar as she ambled across the lush green grass of the backyard.

"*If home is where the heart is . . . if that's what people say . . .*"

Donna could only stare, her eyes wide, her mouth opened into a small O of surprise.

"*I can't feel the rhythm, and I can't hear the rhyme . . .*"

Lark couldn't stop her own feet from tapping, and by the

second chorus, she noticed that her mother's were, too. It wasn't until she heard her own voice singing the final lyrics that Lark realized she had been holding her breath. The music faded away with a close-up of Lark's face against the brilliant blue of the sky.

Then, silence.

Lark waited for her mother to say something. "How could he do such a thing?" would be nice, or maybe "I never saw this coming." Even "What is this?" would have been better than this complete and utter silence.

Lark was about to slink away in shame when Donna slowly turned her head and met Lark's gaze.

That was when Lark saw the tears in her mother's eyes.

"Aidan, may I have a word, please."

Aidan looked up from the computer game he was playing with an expression of innocence on his handsome face. "Something wrong?"

"You bet there is," said Donna.

Lark stood in the doorway of the practice room and watched with a mixture of amazement and satisfaction as her mother crooked her index finger at Aidan. Ollie and Max exchanged glances as their bandmate removed himself from the overstuffed chair and strutted across the room toward Lark's mother.

"In my office. Now."

"That's an awful long walk," said Aidan with an insolent chuckle. "Why don't you just say your piece right here?"

"Fine," said Donna tersely. "What I've got to say is this: you're out."

"Out?" Aidan's careless stance didn't falter. "Out of what?"

"Of his mind," Ollie quipped under his breath.

"Out of luck," Donna retorted. "Out of chances . . . but most of all, out of the band."

"Seriously?" said Max.

Donna continued to glare at Aidan. "I warned you after that sneaking out nonsense that you were on thin ice. And now you go and do . . . this!"

"This?" Ollie echoed. "This what? Bloody hell, Aidan, what have you gone and done now?"

"He stole a song," Lark explained. "From me."

Max looked ready to spit. "You stole a song from Lark? God, Aidan, you're an even bigger jerk than I thought!"

"You can't throw me out," said Aidan, far less relaxed now. "You don't have another keyboard player, remember? What'll you do without me?"

"We'll survive," Donna said coolly.

"You can't prove I stole anything," said Aidan, folding his arms across his chest defiantly.

"As a matter of fact, I can," Donna informed him, holding out Lark's phone and pressing the Play arrow.

As the first few bars of "Homesick" filled the room, Lark was so wrapped up in the drama of the moment that she forgot to feel anxious about the boys hearing her sing.

After the first verse, Donna paused the video. "Is that not the same song you just played for me, claiming you wrote it yourself?"

Aidan looked away and said nothing. It was as good as a confession.

"That's low, Aid," said Ollie with a disgusted shake of his head.

"Oh, and you would know, wouldn't you," Aidan snapped. "Hard to get much lower than stealing a mate's girl."

"I didn't steal your girl," Ollie said, then rolled his eyes and headed for the door. "But it doesn't matter now, does it? Because you're history."

When Ollie was gone, Donna turned a cold look to Aidan. "I've booked you on the next flight to London. A car will be here in exactly one hour to take you to LAX. Your parents have been notified."

"Good," Aidan said. "Because I bet my father's already rung his solicitor. I expect he'll sue you."

"Actually," Donna replied calmly, "I've already called *my* lawyer. Your contract with Lotus Records is being dissolved as we speak. And he's talking to another attorney, one who specializes in intellectual property. The way I see it, Lark can sue *you* for stealing her creative material and attempting to sell it as your own."

Aidan swallowed hard but said nothing.

Donna smiled. "That's what I thought." She gave a toss of her head in the direction of the door. "Now start packing."

CHAPTER FIFTEEN

Tuesday's after-school practice session with Teddy went even better than the day before. Lark sang the refrain—intentionally, this time—and their voices melded together like hot corn bread and honey butter, both great individually, and even sweeter when combined.

When rehearsal was over, Lark felt a twinge of panic. She couldn't avoid walking out with Teddy again, that would be just plain ridiculous. Today she'd have to walk with Teddy across the sprawling school building to get to the late bus. It was a thought she loved and dreaded at the same time. Cursing her shyness, she shouldered her backpack and followed him out of the music room.

"So," he said as they made their way to end of the music corridor, "I was wondering. What's it like living with those British dudes?"

"Eventful," was Lark's immediate response, and it earned her a chuckle from Teddy. "One day I was an only child living in a house that was way too big, and the next, I suddenly had three big brothers crowding me out of all my favorite spaces."

"Big brothers?" Teddy repeated. "That's how it feels?"

"Yep. It feels exactly like having three loud, annoying brothers with giant appetites."

"Oh. So then you don't, you know, have a crush on one of them or anything?"

Lark noticed that Teddy looked away when he asked that question.

"Definitely no crushes," she said.

"Good," Teddy said, then quickly added, "because that would probably be a little weird."

"A lot weird," Lark agreed.

They took the south stairwell to the first floor, then followed the administrative hallway toward the main lobby. At this time of day, the school was mostly empty except for the occasional teacher or custodian passing by. The only other student they saw was Zachary from Lark's math class, waiting outside Principal Hardy's office, miserably clutching a detention notice. Lark wasn't sure if she was relieved or disappointed that none of her classmates were there to see her walking side by side with Teddy Reese.

When they reached the main door, he held it open for

her. It was an old-fashioned, gentlemanly gesture, which she knew her father would have approved of. Mimi would have rolled her eyes.

"They seem like okay guys, and they have a really distinctive sound," Teddy observed. "That kid on keyboards, wow. Last night I tried to teach myself to play some of their songs. They were actually pretty complicated, but man, Aidan made it look easy. I think he might be the most talented musician in the band."

"Funny you should say that," said Lark wryly. "Because he's no longer—"

She stopped talking abruptly when she spotted her mother's SUV at the curb. And leaning beside it was her mom, wearing a long, lightweight trench coat.

And holding Lark's journal.

Lark slid into the passenger seat and waited for her mother to start the car.

"So," Lark said, eyeing the journal, which her mother had laid carefully on top of the dashboard. "You, uh, found it." Lark looked away, embarrassed of what her mother probably read. But she didn't want to hide anymore.

"Well, of course I found it," said Donna, guiding the SUV away from the sidewalk. "You *did* leave it on my pillow last night."

Lark laughed. "Not exactly subtle, huh?"

"No," said Donna, reaching over to pat Lark's knee. "But I'm glad you did it." She slid a sideways glance toward the passenger seat. "I'm going to go out on a limb here and guess that the boy I saw you walking with just now is Teddy, the one you've immortalized in verse?"

"Yep, that's him."

"Well, I can see why he's inspired so many romantic doodles. He's adorable."

Lark's cheeks burned, but it wasn't an entirely unpleasant sensation. "You don't think it's . . . silly? Or dumb?"

"Not at all. I think it's, well, I think it's just as it should be. And a girl needs to be able to confide in her mama about this sort of thing. So thank you for trusting me with your journal. The songs are so moving and powerful! No wonder Aidan tried to steal one."

"About that," said Lark. "What are you going to do now? About Abbey Road, I mean."

Donna sighed, hitting the turn signal and guiding the SUV onto a road Lark had never been on before. "Well, there's a strong precedent for the success of duo acts in the music business, and financially the boys stand to enjoy larger profit margins if they pursue their career without the addition of a third party."

"Sorry, Mom, but I'm not fluent in business jargon. Can you say that again, in English this time?"

"I can launch Max and Ollie as a duet," Donna translated. "But somehow I don't think they'll have the same impact."

Lark agreed. For all his sullenness, Aidan did bring a certain something to the act. She supposed they could always hire a studio musician like her father to fill Aidan's combat boots in recording sessions, but in concert, having an actual band member playing the keyboards would be important. She tried to imagine Ollie and Max onstage as a duet. But talented as they were, there was no denying that the balance would be off without a third performer in the mix.

She was so lost in her thoughts that she didn't notice the drastic change in the scenery that was now speeding past outside her window. The mansions of Beverly Hills and the commercial buildings of Sunset Boulevard had given way to trees and mountains and winding dirt roads.

Donna parked the SUV in a post-and-beam-fenced clearing.

"Where are we?"

"We're as close as we can get to being in the Smoky Mountains without hopping on a plane," her mom answered, getting out of the car.

Lark watched with wide eyes as her mother shed her trench coat to reveal a loose-fitting cotton camp shirt and an old pair of blue jeans. It was an outfit Lark recognized . . . she'd often worn it on the weekends back in Tennessee.

"Boots are in the trunk," said Donna, kicking off her pricey flats and tiptoeing toward the back of the car. "I hope yours still fit."

Lark understood at once. Tugging off her own shoes, she leaped out of the car and joined her mother at the hatchback.

They were going hiking!

"It's magnificent," said Donna, gazing out over the vista of rolling hills and tree-lined valleys. "I'm so glad I took the afternoon off."

"So am I," said Lark, inhaling deeply and letting the fresh mountain air fill her lungs. They'd been trekking the trails of Franklin Canyon Park for almost two hours and, although her leg muscles ached and her cheeks and nose were burned pink, Lark couldn't have been happier. She settled herself on a large rock beside her mother and pulled in another refreshingly clean breath. "We haven't hiked since . . ."

"Since your father and I split up," her mother finished softly. There was a ripple of sadness—or maybe guilt—beneath her words. "Remember that week we camped at Pigeon Forge?"

"Best camping trip ever!" said Lark. "Dad brought his guitar along."

"Of course he did! When did we ever go anywhere and your father *didn't* bring his guitar along?"

"True. But in Pigeon Forge he played by the campfire every night and all the other families who were camping nearby would wander over to join us for a big sing-along."

"Right," said Donna. "I seem to recall I swore if I heard 'Kumbaya' one more time, I'd go jump in the lake."

"But you didn't have to *jump* in the lake, 'cause Daddy threw you in! With all your clothes on! Then he jumped in after you with *his* clothes on and so did I!"

"Yes!" said Donna, laughing. "We looked like three lunatics. Three sopping wet lunatics." She shook her head, smiling at the memory. "It was a great trip."

"Sure was." Lark admired the sun, which was softening to a pinkish hue as it sank toward the distant hilltops. "I wish . . ." But since she wasn't exactly certain what she was wishing for, she finished the thought with a shrug.

Donna reached over and took her daughter's hand. "I'm sorry we haven't been able to do anything fun lately, honey. But getting the record label off the ground has required my full attention."

"I know, Mom. It's okay."

"Tell you what. How about we try to come here at least once a month. I'll make time. We can hike, or just bring a picnic and have dinner while the sun sets. It's no Pigeon Forge, but it will still be nice."

"It will." Lark leaned over to kiss her mother's cheek. "It'll be real nice."

For a moment they just sat quietly, enjoying the view in companionable silence.

"That song Aidan stole from you," Donna broached at last. "It's awfully good."

"Thank you, Mom."

"Does it make me a horrible mother to say that I had no idea you were quite so talented?"

"Not at all!" It was Lark's turn to sound guilty. "It's my fault for not sharing my music with you. I just get so self-conscious."

"Hmmm." Donna gave her a teasing look. "You didn't look especially self-conscious when I saw you walking out of school with Teddy. Maybe that boy brings out the best in you."

"I guess he does," Lark admitted. "In fact, I'm going to play backup guitar for him in the school talent show in a few weeks."

"Lark, that's wonderful! Although in my opinion you're far too gifted to be playing backup for anyone. You should be right up front, playing and singing lead vocals."

"I appreciate your confidence, Mom," said Lark with a sigh. "But I'm not really a 'lead vocals' kind of girl. I'm happy to let other people enjoy the spotlight. Just playing backup for Teddy is taking all the guts I can muster."

Donna gave Lark's hand a squeeze. "I suppose you have to walk before you can run. And the fact that you're performing in public at all means you're getting over your stage fright!"

"Well, not completely," Lark clarified. "I'll play, but I'm not going to actually sing. Except Teddy did talk me into doing a little 'na-na-na-ing' with him."

"Na-na-na-ing?" her mother suddenly looked wary. "What's that? Some new euphemism for making out?"

"Mom!" Lark's eyes went round and her face turned red. "No! It has nothing to do with . . . snogging."

"*Snogging!* What in the world is snogging?"

"Kissing. According to Max. But I promise you, there is absolutely nothing like that going on between Teddy and me. The na-na-nas are in the chorus of the song he's singing in the talent show. I'm going to harmonize with him. Maybe. If I don't chicken out."

Donna let out a sigh of relief. Then she smiled. "Getting back to that song of yours. It really is good. So good, in fact, that I have a business proposition for you. I wanted to record it when I thought Aidan wrote it, and I still want to. It would be a perfect addition to Abbey Road's first album."

Lark's mouth dropped open. "You're kiddin' me."

"I never kid about business, sweet pea," her mother said with a wink.

"You don't think it's too country for them?"

"Well, we might need to make it a bit more pop-y, but there's a lot of cross-over happening these days. I think it's an interesting creative risk. Shows they've got range. And by the way, this would be an official business transaction, which means you'll be paid for the rights, and even earn a royalty."

"Royalties? Honest?"

Donna nodded.

"Can I use the money to buy a car when I turn sixteen?"

"Well, let's see about that when the time comes."

"Maybe I can use the extra money to fly back to Tennessee a lot more often!"

"You could definitely do that," said Donna. "Seeing that 'Homesick' video made me realize how deeply you've been missing Nashville."

"So you won't mind if I try to visit Dad more?"

"Of course I won't mind. Although, you might not have to. At least not right away."

"What do you mean?"

"I heard from your father this morning. His tour has been extended and he's coming to the West Coast. He'll be in California for three whole weeks next month."

For a moment, Lark didn't speak. She didn't move. Then, with a happy squeal she sprang up from the rock and began to dance around, singing at the top of her lungs:

"*Kumbaya, my lord, kumbaya . . .*"

Her joyful voice echoed over the treetops and across the canyon, its lilting echo filling the darkening sky.

Donna laughed, grasping the back of Lark's shirt to keep her from dancing herself off a cliff. "Okay, darlin', I think you've breathed in enough fresh air for now. Time to head back to civilization."

But as they made their way back to the hiking trail, her mother was singing, too.

CHAPTER SIXTEEN

The next several days went by smoothly enough, thanks to the fact that Aidan was gone. Max and Ollie had a true friendship, and a mutual respect for each other's talents. Without the tension created by Aidan's moodiness and jealousy, it was easier for Lark and Donna to get to know their British houseguests, and the more time they spent together, the more they all liked one another. Mrs. Fitzpatrick adored them so much, she let them get away with calling her Fitzy—*and* taught herself to make English-style fish and chips.

While Lark was off at school, the boys met with Jas at his dance studio and learned complicated dance routines, with the choreographer standing in as the nameless "third band member." In the evenings they rehearsed in the music room, minus their keyboard player, which wasn't particularly effective. Lark filled in when her homework allowed, but that was hardly a permanent solution; she was a passable pianist, but as Teddy had pointed out, Aidan was a tough act to follow.

"The situation is getting desperate," Donna said at the breakfast table on Monday morning. Max and Ollie were sleeping in, so it was just Lark and her mother, picking at Mrs. Fitzpatrick's slightly strange mustard and mushroom omelets. "I've already got the studio booked for the band's first recording session and we're short one musician," Donna continued. "I can't cancel, because the booking is non-refundable. I'm afraid the only thing that makes sense is to fly back to London this week to audition new band members."

"London," Lark echoed wistfully, spearing a potato and popping it into her mouth. "That's exciting."

"It is, isn't it?" Donna's fingernails tapped the sides of her coffee mug as she sighed over the rim. "But it's also very expensive, not to mention time-consuming."

"Well," said Lark, "why should you fly all the way to England when we've got Fitzy's fish 'n' chips right here in our own kitchen."

When Donna looked at her daughter as though she'd lost her mind, Lark laughed.

"In other words, you don't need to go to England to replace Aidan. There are thousands of talented teenage boys right here in LA."

Her mother considered this. "You know, you're absolutely right. I was thinking that the third band member had to be British, but that's not written in blood, is it?"

Lark grinned. "Nope."

"Maybe we've just been given a unique opportunity here," Donna said, her enthusiasm growing. "Most boy bands are either all British or all American. But what if we thought outside the box and combined British *and* American talent? It would appeal to fans on both sides of the Atlantic. That would be groundbreaking, right?"

"Right!" said Lark.

Now her mother shifted into music mogul mode. "I'll put out an ad for an open call and we can hold the audition on Saturday. Most of our candidates will be school age, after all, so there's no point in trying to do it on a weekday. I'm sure Jasper will let us use his studio. And of course he'll be part of the selection process." She gave Lark's shoulder a squeeze. "And since it was your idea, it's only right that you are, too!"

"What do you mean?"

"I mean you can help me with the auditions. You're a brilliant songwriter, so you know talent when you hear it, and you also happen to be a card-carrying member of our target demographic. Oh, and let's invite Mimi, too. That girl's got a terrific eye when it comes to this sort of thing."

Lark felt a tingle of excitement. "Thanks, Mom! That'll be fun."

With her satin robe floating behind her like a superhero's cape, Donna dashed to her office to begin making arrangements. Lark wondered briefly if perhaps she should have consulted with Max and Ollie before making such an important decision, but she knew that once her mother got an idea in her head, it was difficult to get her to change her mind.

Luckily, this idea happened to be a good one.

On Saturday, Lark, Mimi, Donna, and the remaining two members of Abbey Road arrived at Jasper's studio to find rock-star hopefuls lined up around the block. It seemed as if every teenage boy in California who'd ever had a music lesson had turned out for the audition.

"Look at them all!" said Mimi, waggling her eyebrows. "You know, I've had dreams like this."

Ollie laughed.

Inside, Jas led them to a large room with high ceilings, wooden floors, and an entire wall of mirrors. He and Donna organized the candidates in the hallway, signing them in and collecting headshots and résumés from those who had them. Mimi quickly set up her video camera on a tripod, while Lark got the music system ready and Ollie and Max warmed up their voices, in case Donna wanted them to sing with anyone. Max set up the electronic keyboard for the boys to play.

Then the six of them sat down at a long table and Donna called out, "Let's begin!"

A boy who looked to be about fourteen stepped into the studio and closed the door behind him.

"The first victim," Max whispered to Lark.

"Shh!" Lark bit back a giggle.

"I feel like a TV talent-show judge!" said Mimi.

Donna consulted the paperwork spread out on the table. "You're Danny Toliver?"

The boy nodded. He had longish, sandy-blond hair and big brown eyes, broad shoulders, and full lips. He certainly looked like a pop star.

Donna nodded to Lark, then Mimi, who began filming.

"Ready, Danny?" asked Lark, feeling indescribably important.

Danny nodded and Lark hit the Play button. The intro to a ballad filled the space. Danny sang the first verse.

He was fabulous! His voice was sweet and raspy and he made such intense eye contact with Lark that her heart began to race. She could easily imagine legions of screaming girls chasing this boy down the street.

When he finished singing, "the judging panel" applauded.

"Very nice, Danny," said Donna, making some notes.

"Do you have any dance experience?" Jas inquired.

Danny Toliver gave them the cockiest grin Lark had ever seen. "Nothing formal," he said, "but I've got some moves."

"Let's see them then, mate," urged Ollie, reaching across Lark to once again cue the music.

Danny's "moves" looked less like a dance combination than the reaction of a person in the throes of being electrocuted! His arms shot out, then darted back in, jerking and flailing with no respect for tempo whatsoever, while his legs quivered and his head bobbled. Then he began to spin, faster and faster.

"He looks like somebody put him in a blender," Mimi observed under her breath.

"I'm getting seasick just watching him," quipped Ollie.

In a show of mercy, Jasper hit the Off button. The music stopped instantaneously, but unfortunately it took Danny Toliver a little longer to come to a halt, which he did by colliding with the tripod. Both dancer and camera went crashing to the ground.

Mimi let out a yelp and ran to check on her most prized possession. Donna ran to check on Danny.

"Are you hurt?"

"Hurt?" Danny looked up from the floor and gave her that cocky smile. "No way. That's what rock 'n' roll is all about."

"That's what safety helmets are all about," murmured Ollie. "But hey, I say sign him up. He actually makes *my* dancing look *good*."

Donna let out a heavy sigh. "Next!" she called.

The second boy introduced himself as Nick Campanelli. Nick was a dark-haired, god-like young man, with rippling muscles and chiseled features. His personality was a flirtatious mix of shyness and charm.

And his voice . . . his voice . . .

"Is he singing?" Max whispered. "Or has his appendix just burst?"

"Next!"

After Nick came Miles; after Miles came Caleb; after Caleb came Ethan; and after every single one of them came Donna's voice shouting out, "*Next!*"

And with every shout, the hopes of the judging panel dropped a little bit more.

By the time they got to Jared Bleeth, Donna had begun to sound panicked.

Jared Bleeth was an athletic fifteen-year-old whose voice was nothing short of a miracle. He could shift from rock to opera without missing a beat. He was a keyboard prodigy, and he'd studied every form of dance from ballet to hip-hop since he was old enough to walk. On top of that, with his twinkling blue eyes and light-brown curls, Jared Bleeth was almost too handsome to look at.

"That smile," breathed Mimi. "It's dazzling."

"It's like looking directly into the sun," Lark agreed.

When Jared finished his song, Donna quickly consulted with the others, then leaped to her feet. "Bravo!" she exclaimed, clapping. "Jared, welcome to Abbey Road."

"Really?" Jared knocked them out with his stunning smile. "That's awesome. I just have one concern."

"What's that, mate?" asked Ollie.

"Well, I won't be able to record during the last few weeks of January."

"Oh, we can work around your schedule," Donna assured him. "I assume you've got school commitments?"

"Not exactly," said Jared. "I just need to be at home to, you know, prepare."

"Prepare for what?" asked Max.

"Dude, haven't you heard? They've deciphered a prehistoric calendar, which predicts a ninety-eight-point-five percent probability that aliens from an as-yet undiscovered planet will attack the earth in the middle of February. I'll need at least a few weeks to get ready for battle. I'm gonna kick some interplanetary butt!"

Mimi's mouth dropped open. Ollie shook his head and Max groaned and covered his face with his hands. Donna and Jas exchanged looks of disbelief, while Lark held her breath, waiting for the punch line.

But there wasn't one. Jared clearly believed every word he'd said, which meant that despite his sizzling good looks and heart-melting singing voice, Jared Bleeth was also a total nut job!

Lark let out her breath in a heavy sigh of disappointment. And six desperate and exhausted voices called out in unison:

"*NEXT!*"

By five o'clock, Lark was ready to call it quits. She couldn't believe she'd actually been looking forward to this.

Most of the boys had the right look—wholesomely handsome with a dash of mischief in their eyes, trendy haircuts, hip clothing. But there were a few that had Lark wondering if perhaps maybe Jared had been right about the aliens invading . . . except they'd turned up earlier than expected.

One boy, who called himself Ink, was so covered in tattoos that he looked like a building that had been vandalized with graffiti. Another kid had shaved half his head and wore his remaining hair in multicolored dreadlocks; yet another had an earring in each nostril and wore a dog collar with a leash. On the opposite end of the spectrum was a bespectacled boy in an argyle sweater and bow tie who wore his hair parted neatly on the side and greased into place like a 1950s businessman. Based on his appearance, his earsplitting, punk-rock rendition of "God Bless America" came as a bit of a shock.

Then there was the boy in the traditional Scottish kilt who seemed promising until he dared Lark to guess what he was wearing underneath his tartan. Jas showed him the door—fast.

By the end of the day they'd asked only three performers to remain for a second interview.

"Lark, you and Mimi don't have to stay for the callbacks," said Donna wearily. "I just want to see how these three interact with Max and Ollie, to test whether there's any chemistry."

"If there is, I'll bet it's a toxic explosion," said Mimi, gathering her camera equipment.

Donna managed a halfhearted laugh. But the truth of the matter was that if they didn't find someone talented— and normal—enough to replace Aidan, they would have to reinvent Abbey Road as a duo. And that was far from ideal.

"I've called a car for you," said Donna. "It's waiting out front." Then she kissed Lark on the forehead and rolled her eyes. "Have Mrs. Fitzpatrick keep dinner warm for the rest of us. Something tells me this could take a while."

"I'll walk you out," Max offered, carrying Mimi's tripod.

"Are you sure you're not a duke or an earl or something?" Mimi asked, grinning. "Because your manners rock."

"Yeah, that's me," Max said. "The Duke of Camden Town." Then he muttered something that Lark thought sounded like, "And I wish I could go back."

Downstairs, as Mimi loaded her camera equipment into the trunk of the car, Lark pulled Max aside.

"You okay?" she asked softly.

"I dunno." Max shrugged. "Today was a bit of a letdown."

Lark wished she could argue with him. "I'm sorry about that."

"Not your fault," said Max, tapping her chin in a brotherly manner. "But just between us, I think maybe it was Aidan who got lucky. I'd give just about anything to be home in England right now."

Lark's heart plummeted to her feet. "No! Please don't say that. You have to stay. Ollie needs you. It means so much to my mother." She put her hands on his shoulders and gave a squeeze. "It means a lot to me, too."

"Thanks," said Max, "but it feels like Abbey Road is doomed."

"Promise me you won't do anything drastic," said Lark, giving his shoulders a little shake. "Just stay a few more weeks, okay? It might all work out. And if it does, you'll be on top of the world. You told me yourself, your family could use the extra income. But if you quit and go home now, you'll never know what could have happened."

Max was quiet for a long moment. Then he smiled. "Okay, Lark. For both of our families, I'll tough it out a bit longer."

Mimi closed the trunk and got in the car. Lark slid into the backseat after her, quickly rolling down the rear window to give Max a wave and an encouraging smile.

"Maybe one of the boys we've called back will surprise you," she said hopefully.

"Not sure how anything could be more surprising than dog collars and aliens," Max said with a chuckle, "but I like your optimism."

Lark rolled up the window. Max didn't share her positive attitude, but at least he'd agreed to stay just a little bit longer.

With any luck, that was all it would take.

CHAPTER SEVENTEEN

On Sunday, Lark spent the day with Max and Ollie by the pool, where they filled her in on everything that had happened after she and Mimi had left the studio.

According to Max and Ollie, the boys who'd been offered second interviews had failed to impress in an epic fashion. One had come right out and told them that his ultimate goal was to become a solo act, so he'd only be joining the band as a temporary first step in his career—if they wanted to sign him, he could give them a year, tops.

The second contender had wanted to talk about only one thing: money. Would the band's earnings be divided equally among the three of them, or should he, as the newcomer, expect a smaller cut? What was Donna's fee? Who would be overseeing their investments?

The third hopeful was simply too full of himself. He was conceited, self-centered, and just plain rude. His fatal error was asking Donna if she could set him up with the hot little redhead who'd been working the sound system.

"Don't call us," Donna had snarled, strutting across the room to fling open the door. "We'll call you."

The fact that the auditions had been such a failure put Lark in a grim mood to start the week. Monday seemed to drag by. The only thing that made it bearable was the knowledge that right after the last bell, she'd be meeting Teddy in the music room to rehearse.

Her last period class—English—was nearly boring her to tears. The teacher was droning on about Apollo, or maybe it was Aphrodite, but try as she might, Lark just couldn't stop replaying the disastrous auditions over and over in her head.

Which was why she almost didn't notice the note slide quietly across her desk.

This was weird in the extreme. The only person who ever wrote her notes was Mimi, and Mimi wasn't in this class. Lark glanced at the desk to her left, the direction from which the note had been delivered.

C. J. Bailey, Teddy's soccer teammate and best friend, was smiling at her.

"From Reese," he whispered.

Lark opened the note, hoping her hand wouldn't tremble.

Bad news. Saunders needs the music room for a tuba lesson today. We'll have to find

*another place to rehearse. I'll meet you at
your locker.*

Teddy

The only thing that could have made it better was if
he'd actually signed the letter "Love, Teddy." But the fact
that he knew the location of her locker was a pretty good
trade-off.

After class, Lark hurried through the crowded hallways
to her locker. Teddy was already waiting there.

"Hi."

"Hi."

"Can't believe we got bumped from the rehearsal room."
He sighed and ran a hand through his thick hair. "I asked the
wrestling coach if we could use the auxiliary gym, but the
team has a match today."

"Probably a good thing," said Lark, sliding her English
textbook into her locker. "That gym always smells like sweat
socks."

Teddy laughed. "I'd say we could go to my house, but
my mom has her book club today. Twelve ladies crying
over some slushy romance? Not exactly optimal rehearsal
conditions."

"Barely even suboptimal," Lark agreed.

"So . . ."

"So . . ."

Lark stared into her locker; Teddy shuffled his feet. Around them, the end-of-the-day chaos seemed to fade to silence. If they couldn't come up with an alternate venue, they were going to have to cancel their rehearsal for the day. Lark would rather sell her soul than allow that to happen, and unless it was her imagination, she had a feeling Teddy felt the same way. Because of the talent show, of course. But still . . .

Lark summoned up all of her courage and suggested, "We can go to my house."

"Really?" Teddy's face brightened. "That would be great. And you can use your own guitar."

"Right. That's what I was thinking." *Liar.* What Lark had really been thinking was that from that moment on she could say that Teddy Reese had been in her house. "So we're on, then?"

"Def. I've just gotta run to my locker. What bus are you on?"

"Seventeen. It's usually the third one in line in the east lot."

"Cool. Meet you there." He turned to walk away, then turned back and grinned. "Save me a seat?"

Lark felt her knees wobble. "Well, I was thinking we'd just strap you to the roof, but I guess the seat thing works, too."

Teddy cracked up all the way down the hall, which pleased Lark immensely. She immediately texted Mimi and filled her in, right down to the joke about the bus roof.

Since when did I get so witty?

184

Mimi typed back, adding a thumbs-up emoji. **Maybe Ollie's rubbing off on you.**

Lark responded with a laughing face, then tucked her phone into her backpack.

It wasn't until she was on the bus that she remembered something: Ollie and Max didn't have dance rehearsal today, which meant they'd be there when she got home . . . with Teddy!

As she sunk into the bus seat, she knew that the tumble of nerves she was experiencing was probably what every girl felt the first time she brought home a friend of the opposite sex. She was pretty sure that Ollie and Max would tease and torment her about Teddy's visit.

Surprisingly, she realized that she didn't care. She'd begun to think of Ollie and Max as her big brothers, and teasing was what big brothers did.

Lark spotted Teddy climbing the bus steps and when he caught sight of her, he smiled.

In that moment Lark decided that no matter how many jokes and comments Ollie and Max made about Lark having a crush, it would be totally worth it.

The kitchen smelled of melted chocolate mixed with warm butter and sugar. The counters were cluttered with half-empty egg cartons and cans of baking powder, and there was a cooling rack on the center island that held at least two dozen cookies.

Lark smiled; she'd picked a good day to invite someone over.

"Mrs. Fitzpatrick?"

The housekeeper didn't look up from the counter, where she was rolling out more cookie dough. "Yes, dear?"

"Um . . . I was wondering if my friend and I could have a snack?"

"No need to be shy! Since when do you and Mimi need permission to raid the refrigerator?"

"Well, um, it's not Mimi. It's Teddy."

This got the housekeeper's attention! Mrs. Fitzpatrick snapped her gaze up from the floury countertop and adjusted her glasses to peer at the young man standing beside Lark in the kitchen doorway.

"Well, well. Hello, Teddy. Welcome."

"Hello."

"This is Mrs. Fitzpatrick," said Lark. "And you are about to have the best chocolate chip cookies you've ever tasted." She was thankful that her housekeeper had decided to play it safe today—her basil and bacon brownies earlier in the week hadn't been a success. Even the boys had refused to eat them.

Mrs. Fitzpatrick was already selecting the most perfect cookies from the batch and arranging them on a plate. "Still warm."

"Thanks," said Teddy, accepting the cookies and breathing in the heavenly aroma. "Wow. These smell incredible."

"Secret recipe," Lark informed him in a stage whisper. "She won't tell a soul what she does to it, but I think she doubles the butter or triples the sugar."

"My guess would be both," said Teddy, taking a bite. The look on his face was pure joy. "And from the taste of it, I'd say she quadruples the chocolate chips!"

Lark giggled. "You might be on to something."

"Milk?" Mrs. Fitzpatrick offered, rushing toward the fridge.

"No, thanks," said Lark, breaking off a small piece of cookie and popping it daintily into her mouth. "We're going to rehearse, and you're supposed to avoid dairy before you sing. It coats your vocal cords."

"Is that true?" asked Teddy.

Lark shrugged. "Well, my dad swears by it."

"Sing?" said Mrs. Fitzpatrick. "Who's going to sing?"

"We are," said Lark. "Teddy and I are performing in the talent show and we have to practice."

"What's this about a talent show?"

Lark turned to see Max and Ollie coming down the back stairs from the practice room. When Ollie reached the bottom and spotted Teddy standing beside Lark, he stopped in his tracks, causing Max to crash into him from behind.

"I knew the smell of cookies would bring you rascals down here," said Mrs. Fitzpatrick with a satisfied smirk. "Now, all of you, out of my kitchen. I have more baking to do. I'll bring some cookies upstairs for you later, to snack on while you rehearse."

"So that's it?" asked Max, eyeing Lark. "You two are rehearsing for your school talent show?"

"Yep," said Teddy, smiling sheepishly. "I guess that sounds pretty small-time to you guys, huh?"

"Not at all, mate," said Ollie, giving him a friendly clap on the shoulder. "How do you think we got started?"

"We'd be happy to give you a few pointers," Max offered. "If you're interested."

"That would be great," said Teddy. "I mean, if it's okay with Lark." He turned a hopeful look in her direction. "I know you've got that whole stage fright thing, but maybe having a small audience would be good practice."

"He's right," said Ollie.

"Baby steps," Max agreed. "Besides, it's just us. We're practically family, right?"

Lark bit her lip. A mild tingle of panic wound its way up her spine, but it was nothing compared to what she usually felt when she thought about singing in public. She supposed that was an improvement. Max and Ollie weren't strangers anymore. Maybe she could do it. And Teddy was right, she needed to get used to having people listen to her.

"Okay," she said. "But go easy on us!"

"Never," said Ollie.

"Forget it!" said Max.

"Good." Teddy laughed. "A little constructive criticism never killed anybody."

Lark slid a glance at Max and Ollie, and seeing the mischievous looks in their eyes, she sincerely hoped she wasn't making a huge mistake.

They performed Teddy's song just as they'd done in the music room at school.

Lark's and Teddy's voices combined flawlessly for the final "yeah," then faded away as Lark strummed the last chord.

Silence followed. And then . . .

Both boys were on their feet, applauding!

"That was ace!"

"Wicked!"

Ollie darted across the room to give Teddy a fist bump. "You've got pipes, mate!"

"Thanks."

"No, seriously," said Max. "You can sing. You're as good as Ollie."

To Lark's delight, Teddy blushed. "Well, I wouldn't say that."

"Neither would I," joked Ollie. "But that doesn't mean it isn't true."

As if he suddenly remembered she was in the room, Max turned to Lark. "Oh, and you were great, too, Lark. Nice one."

Lark smiled. It was clearly an afterthought, but she didn't mind. Teddy was the one who'd done most of the singing, after all, and she could tell this praise from the older boys meant the world to him.

"Do you play an instrument?" Ollie asked.

By way of response, Teddy positioned himself at the keyboard and played the Beatles' "Let It Be."

Max's eyes went wide.

Ollie's brows shot up. "Okay, who are you really, and what have you done with Paul McCartney?"

Teddy laughed. "That's pretty much the best compliment I've ever gotten."

"Seems there's no end to your talent," Max observed.

"You should see him play soccer," said Lark.

At this, Max and Ollie exchanged a look.

"I think you mean football," Ollie corrected. "Doesn't matter. Just tell me there's a ball somewhere in that garage of yours."

"Well, yeah, there is, but—"

"Come on, then," said Max, dropping an arm around Teddy's shoulders. "Let's put that huge lawn to good use. We haven't had a decent kickabout since we got here. Oi, Ollie, where did I leave my trainers?"

"Wait!" said Lark. "What are y'all doing? Teddy and I have to rehearse. The talent show is Friday night!"

Laughing, Ollie took her face in his hands and planted a loud kiss in the middle of her forehead. "All work and no play . . . you know how that goes. Come on! You can be in goal."

"But the song—"

"Is already brilliant. Now go change into something you don't mind getting mucky, because when Maxie and I play football, we show no mercy."

For the next two hours, it was Lark and Max versus Ollie and Teddy. The boys were as impressed with Teddy's fancy footwork as they were with his singing and piano playing. They were quick to congratulate Lark, who'd only played two years of youth soccer back in Nashville, for holding her own.

When Teddy scored for the fourth time, Ollie gave him a high five. "I'm surprised you haven't already been signed by LA Galaxy," he teased.

"So," said Max, scooping up the soccer ball and tucking it under his arm, "I'm thinking that if your moves on the pitch are this good, your moves on the dance floor must be pretty slick as well."

Teddy grinned. "That sounds like a challenge."

They all trooped into the pratice room above the garage. The following hour was spent demonstrating Jasper's dance combinations for Teddy to see how quickly he could pick them up. *Very* quickly, it turned out.

Finally Teddy held up his hands in surrender. "This was awesome," he said, catching his breath. "But my mom's gonna be here in a few minutes." He looked disappointed about leaving.

"Don't forget your backpack," said Lark. "Fitzy probably put it in my bedroom."

As Teddy followed her out of the room, Lark prayed the boys wouldn't make any goofy remarks about the two of them going off alone together.

"They're really down-to-earth," Teddy confided as they headed down the hall. "They don't have an attitude at all."

"Yeah," said Lark. "I can tell they think you're cool, too."

When Lark opened the door to her bedroom, she felt a surge of panic, hoping she hadn't left anything embarrassing lying around. Luckily, there weren't any unmentionables dangling from the bedpost.

"Cool room," said Teddy, glancing around and taking in the framed photo of Lark and Jackson, which she kept on her nightstand. "Is this your dad?"

"Yep. He lives in Nashville. He's a country musician."

"That's so awesome."

Lark smiled. "I think so, too. But I'm so used to people around here turning up their noses at country music. Like, they think every country song ever written is about some mopey cowboy crying into his beer about his cheating wife, or his lost hound dog, or the big dent in his new red pickup truck."

Teddy laughed. "I like some country stuff," he said. "Like Taylor Swift."

"Taylor isn't a hundred percent country anymore," Lark corrected. "She writes some pretty amazing songs."

"Do you write your own songs, too?" Teddy asked.

"Well, actually . . ."

Summoning all her courage, Lark picked up a page of sheet music from her desk and handed it to Teddy.

Teddy took the page with reverence. "'Is It Just Me?'" he read. "Great title."

"Thanks."

He scanned the lyrics, hummed a few bars, and then *he* began to sing the song!

Lark thought her heart might burst. Teddy's voice was perfect for her song, and hearing him sing the words she'd written practically made her dizzy.

When he was finished, he looked up from the music with an expression of admiration. "Wow. You really wrote this, huh? It's incredible."

"You sang it perfectly."

Teddy smiled. "The lyrics are so true. It's how I feel every day."

He had to be kidding, didn't he? Teddy Reese had the whole school in the palm of his hand. Or so it had always seemed to Lark. "You do?"

"Yeah. I think everybody does, at least at our age, anyway. Some kids put up a good front, but inside we all feel like dorks once in a while." He laughed. "Okay, more than once in a while. But that's what's so cool about these lyrics. They make you feel connected, less alone."

Lark didn't know what to say. It was the best review she could have imagined. For a moment, they just stood there, smiling at each other.

Finally, the sound of a car horn broke the silence.

"That's my mom," said Teddy, shouldering his backpack.

Lark walked Teddy to the driveway, where he introduced her to his mother through the open window of the station wagon.

"You're as cute as my mother-in-law said you were," Mrs. Reese said, offering Lark a sweet smile. "We're all thrilled that you're going to perform with Teddy in the talent show."

"So am I," said Lark, hoping she sounded more confident than she actually felt. *I wonder how thrilled they'll be if I walk onto that stage and pass out from stage fright. Or wet my pants...*

Teddy's voice broke through her gloomy imaginings.

"See you tomorrow, Lark. Rehearsal in the music room, as usual, right?"

"Right."

Lark watched the car drive away before practically floating back into the house. Ollie and Max were waiting in the foyer, both still flushed from dancing and filthy from their soccer game. They were smiling like a couple of five-year-olds.

Lark braced herself. "Okay," she said, sighing. "Let me have it."

"Lark's got a boyfriend!" Ollie crooned.

Max batted his eyelashes and made kissing sounds.

"Hilarious," said Lark.

"We heard him singing to you," said Ollie.

"Yeah," said Max with a wink. "You know things are getting serious when a boy serenades you with your own original song. I think it means you're heading down the aisle."

"Stop it," said Lark, biting back a smile. "It's not like that. We're friends."

"Please!" said Ollie. "That boy fancies you. Trust me."

"He does not."

"Does too!"

"Whatever!" Rolling her eyes, Lark headed for the stairs as Ollie and Max broke into a chorus of "Here Comes the Bride."

CHAPTER EIGHTEEN

Lark was nearly asleep when she heard a gentle knock on her bedroom door.

"Lark, honey? You awake?"

"Yes, Mom." Lark sat up and turned on the bedside lamp. "Come on in."

An exhausted-looking Donna pushed open the door, tiptoed across the room, and dropped onto the edge of Lark's bed. "Just wanted to kiss you good night and see how your day was. I heard you had a visitor."

"Teddy came over to rehearse."

"Wish I'd been here to meet him."

"Me too. But I can introduce y'all after the talent show on Friday night."

Donna's reply was lost in a yawn.

"Any luck finding a replacement for Aidan?" Lark asked, although she already had a pretty good idea of the answer.

"Unfortunately, no. I called every talent scout, vocal coach, and school for the performing arts in the greater Los Angeles area. I even reached out to an agent I know in New York, but he only has a handful of clients in this age range, and they're all currently booked on Broadway."

"I'm sorry, Mom."

"I did have high hopes for one boy I heard about from Sacramento . . . or maybe it was Santa Monica. Anyway, he's been singing jingles for television commercials since he was six. So I got in touch with his manager . . . correction, his '*mom*-ager.'" Donna shook her head in exasperation. "What a nightmare! She wanted a guarantee in writing that her son would be paid double whatever Ollie and Max earn because he already has 'professional recording credits.' I told her that the 'Canine Crispies' dog treats jingle certainly didn't entitle him to top billing in a pop act. So *she* turned *me* down, if you can believe it! Honestly. That poor kid. Can you imagine having such a cutthroat businesswoman for a mother?"

"Hmm, let me think . . ."

Donna gave her a playful slap on the arm. "Ha-ha. Very funny!"

"I'm just kidding," Lark said, laughing. "But seriously, what are you going to do about the band?"

"I really don't know. But I don't want you to worry. You just concentrate on the talent show and that adorable singing partner of yours, Freddy."

"Teddy," Lark corrected. In the next second, she sat up and shouted, "Teddy!"

"Okay, okay . . . ," said Donna. "I'm too tired to think straight. I *meant* Teddy."

"No, Mom, you don't understand."

"So his name *isn't* Teddy?" asked Donna, confused.

"His name *is* Teddy . . . and *he* can replace Aidan in Abbey Road!"

Donna considered this for all of three seconds, then shook her head.

"Why not?" demanded Lark.

"Well, first of all, Teddy's never been in a band."

"So? Neither has the boy who sings the Critter Crunchies jingle."

"Canine Crispies."

"Whatever. *He* didn't have any real band experience and you would have taken *him*. It's a perfect plan. Aidan and Ollie hung out with Teddy all afternoon and they got along great, plus they think he's super talented. And you should hear him on the keyboard, Mom. He's almost as good as Aidan was."

"But isn't Teddy your age?"

"He's thirteen."

Donna shook her head. "He's still awfully young, Lark. Ollie's fifteen, and Max is fourteen and a half. I know it doesn't sound like much, but maturity-wise, a few years can make a big difference." She gave Lark an apologetic look.

"Besides, what makes you think Teddy would want to give up his normal life to become a rock star?"

"Because this is America. That's what everybody wants!"

"Not you."

This brought Lark up short. Her mother was right—Lark had been avoiding the spotlight her whole life. But somehow, she just knew that Teddy would welcome the opportunity.

"He's the one, Mom," Lark insisted. "Just give him a chance."

"Lark," said Donna wearily, "I appreciate your help, but isn't it possible that you're just a little bit biased when it comes to Teddy? Maybe you're not exactly an impartial judge."

"Okay, then judge for yourself," said Lark, feeling hopeful now. She knew the minute her mother heard Teddy sing, she'd sign him in a heartbeat. "You'll hear him sing on Friday. Then you'll know I'm right."

Donna rubbed her eyes. "About that, honey. I don't think I'm going to be able to make it Friday night. I'm planning to fly to Chicago to set up some auditions there."

Lark blinked. "You're going to miss my talent show?" It felt like a punch to the gut.

"It wasn't an easy decision," said Donna. "But the situation is getting desperate. And I've heard you play the guitar a million times. You said it yourself—you're not singing lead vocals, you're just playing accompaniment for Teddy.

And as proud as I am of you for finding the courage to do that—"

The lie was out before Lark could stop herself. "I'm singing."

"You're what?"

"I'm singing. I wasn't going to at first. I was just going to play backup, but after our hike and everything you said about me belonging in the spotlight, I changed my mind. It was going to be a surprise, but I'm going to sing my new song 'Is It Just Me?' live, in front of the whole school. And I really need you to be there when I do. I swear I won't be able to get through it without you in the audience."

Donna's tired face brightened. "Lark, that's wonderful. Well, of course I'll be there. I can go to Chicago on Saturday. I wouldn't miss your solo performance for the world." She kissed Lark and crossed the room. "Good night, baby."

"Good night, Mom. And thanks for changing your plans. You have no idea how much it means to me."

Lark waited until her mother closed the bedroom door behind her. Then she turned out the light and whispered into the darkness, "And how much it's going to mean to Teddy."

The next day at lunch, over salads and breadsticks, Lark told Mimi what she'd done.

"So let me get this straight," said Mimi, popping a cherry tomato into her mouth. "Three weeks ago your biggest fear in the world was performing in public, but *now* you're not only accompanying Teddy in the talent show, you're also *singing a solo*?"

"Pretty much," said Lark, taking a sip of her chocolate milk. "It was the only way I could be sure my mother would come to the show. She has to hear Teddy sing or she'll never even consider putting him in the band."

"He's that good, huh?"

"He's terrific. The thing is, it really didn't hit me that I was actually going to be singing in front of the whole school until I saw my name on the sign-up sheet, right beneath 'Howie Dornbaum, Magician.'"

"Hmm," said Mimi, crunching into a green pepper. "Maybe you can ask Howie if he knows any tricks to make your stage fright disappear."

Lark laughed in spite of her mood. "I'd rather he make *me* disappear."

"You're going to be great," Mimi assured her.

"I'm glad you feel that way. Because I kind of have a favor to ask you."

"Name it," said Mimi.

Lark smiled. "I was hoping you might be willing to put together a new video for me."

Mimi's eyes were gleaming. "I'm listening."

"Well, I was thinking that maybe you could put together a montage of all the videos you've ever taken of me singing."

"No problem," said Mimi. "But what do you want it for?"

"To use as part of my act," Lark explained. "It would be a cool way for us to team up, to share the spotlight together. See, while I'm performing the song onstage, we can project your video montage on the big screen behind me. It'll look cool, and it might divert some of the attention away from the real *live* me singing on the stage." She gave her friend a guilty look. "I know you wanted to enter a video in the show all along, and I really should have said yes right from the start. You're always so supportive of me, and I was wrong to let my fear ruin it for you."

"I was a little upset at first," Mimi admitted. "But I know you're really, truly scared. I totally understand that."

"All the more reason for me to help you let your talent shine. So will you do it?"

"Of course! It'll be just like at a real concert, where they show the performance on the Jumbotron for the people in the cheap seats."

"It's the caf-a-gym-a-torium," Lark said, laughing. "*All* the seats are cheap!"

"I've already got a million ideas for special effects," said Mimi, and Lark could practically see the wheels in her head spinning. "It'll be amazing. Your voice, my cinematic vision . . . we're gonna make an awesome team!"

Lark threw her arms around Mimi and hugged her. "We already do, Meems! We already do!"

CHAPTER
NINETEEN

The rest of the week was a blur.

The good news was that Teddy's song got better every time they practiced it.

The bad news was that Lark was getting more and more scared. Over the past few weeks she'd made significant progress toward overcoming her fear of performing in public. Playing guitar at the sing-along with Holly Rose, filling in on the keyboards after Aidan's departure, and harmonizing with Teddy on the chorus had been huge strides for her, but as the talent show approached, that newfound courage was swiftly fading. The more she imagined herself onstage in front of her classmates and their families, the more she whipped herself into a panic.

On Thursday night, Lark couldn't sleep. She lay in bed staring at the outfits she and Mimi had picked out for her to wear in the talent show: dark jeans and a simple black sweater for her performance with Teddy; faded jeans with rips in the knees and a blousy peasant top with colorful embroidery around the neckline for her solo.

"Country chic," Mimi had deemed it. "You'll be gorgeous. We'll do your hair up. Wispy tendrils. Dangling earrings."

And of course, her cowboy boots.

"They're going to think I'm a visitor from another planet," Lark had protested.

"Planet Nashville," Mimi had joked. "It all works. Trust me."

"I do trust you," Lark had replied. "It's having faith in myself where I run into trouble."

It was now well after midnight, and Lark was no closer to dozing off. Tossing aside the covers, she got out of bed and slipped into her boots, then tiptoed downstairs and out the kitchen door.

It was a beautiful night, balmy and starry. *Funny*, thought Lark, settling herself on a poolside lounge chair, *the stars that twinkle over Nashville are the exact same ones that shine above Beverly Hills.*

Of course, in Nashville, you couldn't see the lights of LA. From the pool patio, the city looked like an enormous constellation that had chosen to descend from the sky to sparkle here on earth.

Or maybe it hadn't chosen; maybe it had fallen! Crashed and burned!

Just like Lark was going to do tomorrow night.

She closed her eyes, trying to picture herself singing to an audience that included Alessandra Drake and her cronies. On the upside, nice kids like Emma DiGiorgio, Jessica Ferris, and Duncan Breslow would be there as well. Mr. Saunders, too. Plus the boys, Mimi and Mrs. Reese, and most importantly, her mom.

So the numbers were in her favor. More friends than enemies.

But that didn't make the prospect any less terrifying.

And speaking of terrifying, what was that shadow, moving by the pool house?

Lark's breath seized in her chest.

There was an intruder in the yard!

Trembling, Lark rose from the lounge chair and picked up the pool skimmer to use as a weapon.

But then she heard a British accent. The "intruder" was speaking into a cell phone.

"Wish I could be there with you today," he was saying. "Eat some candy floss and rock for me."

Max! Lark dropped the pool skimmer and nearly crumpled to the grass with relief. When he emerged from the shadows and saw her, he jumped.

"Whoa! What's this? What are you doing out at this hour?"

"I was just going to ask you the same question," Lark shot back.

"I wanted to ring my little sister in London and I didn't want to wake anyone up, that's all. It's her thirteenth birthday today. The whole family's heading up to Brighton to celebrate, and I'm missing it." He shook his head. "I dunno, Lark. I'm really feeling like it's time for me to go home."

Lark wanted to argue with him. She wanted to remind him that even though they still hadn't replaced Aidan, the band had a bright future. She wanted to talk him out of going back to the places and people he loved, but she knew that would make her the world's biggest hypocrite.

Because it was exactly what she wanted to do.

"I'd go with you," she said, "if it would get me out of singing tomorrow night."

"Stop. You're going to be brilliant." He gave her a grin. "I used to get nervous when we started out, but I came up with the perfect cure for stage fright."

Lark rolled her eyes. "I bet you're going to tell me you pictured the audience in their underwear, right?"

"Nope. I pictured the audience in *my* underwear. Much weirder!"

"Ewww!" Lark laughed.

"Quite. So you just go out there and imagine the whole crowd turned out in your knickers. Just be sure they wash them before they give 'em back."

"Gross!"

"Totes. But look, you aren't scared anymore, are you?"

"Well, I'm not scared *now*," Lark conceded. "But I can't say for sure it's going to last until tomorrow night."

Max's eyes turned serious. "I'll tell you what. If you promise me you'll try your very best on that stage tomorrow night, I'll stick around a little longer . . ."

He held out his smartphone. On the screen was an e-ticket to Heathrow.

Lark felt tears prickle behind her eyes. "Max . . . no."

"Sorry, Lark. I'm just not sure we're ever going to find someone to take Aidan's place."

"But I've found someone!"

"Who?"

She smiled. "Teddy!"

Suddenly, Max was smiling, too. "You know, he might just work."

"He *will* work," Lark insisted. "I've just got to get Mom on board. I'm sure she'll be all for it as soon as she sees him perform."

"Which can't happen unless you perform with him," Max pointed out. "So let's get you inside before you catch a cold. Can't have you harmonizing with a nose full of boogers!"

"Ewww!"

"Exactly."

As they made their way back to the house, Max took Lark's hand and gave it an affectionate squeeze. "You know, if I can't have my kid sister around to torture over boyfriends and boogers and dirty knickers, I'm really glad I have you to tease."

It didn't sound like much of a compliment, but in her heart Lark knew it was one of the sweetest ones she'd ever heard.

Despite Max's advice, on Friday Lark was right back to where she'd started on the stage fright scale. She was relieved when Teddy suggested they cancel rehearsal to rest their voices for that night's performance.

At home she tried to nap, but the best she could manage was a fitful half sleep, in which she dreamed of being laughed off the stage by a bunch of strangers wearing pink camisoles and white cotton panties!

Finally, it was time to get ready for the show. Mimi came over to help Lark with her makeup. This was a treat, since Donna normally only allowed Lark to wear pastel lip gloss on the weekends. Mimi kept it simple, with just enough smoky eye shadow, blush, and lipstick to keep Lark from looking invisible onstage.

Not that she wouldn't have loved a little invisibility right about now.

When Mimi had completed what she called her "master-piece," they went downstairs to join Donna and the boys in the foyer.

"Blimey!" said Max.

"You look stunning," said Ollie. "If I didn't know you, I'd think you were at least fifteen. Maybe even sixteen."

"Which is why she's not usually allowed to wear makeup," said Donna pointedly. Her tone was stern, but she was smiling. "You look beautiful, baby girl. Mimi, excellent job. I'll see you all in the—what do you call it? The gym-a-caf-a-brary-playground-atorium?"

"Close enough," joked Mimi. "Your seats are right next to my parents'. Third row, center."

"Wait," said Lark, panicking. "Mama, aren't you driving us?"

"Mrs. Fitzpatrick will take you," said Donna, kissing the top of Lark's head. "I've got to, um, I've got a meeting. But it's on the way. So don't worry, I'll be there in plenty of time to hear you sing."

Hearing Lark sing had never been the point. It was Teddy her mother needed to hear. And because he'd signed up early, he'd be performing early in the show, unlike Lark, who'd be last.

Car keys jangling, Donna wished Lark good luck and hurried out the door.

Lark thought she might cry.

"Okay," said Mimi. "Let's be sure we've got everything we need. Video? Check. Guitar? Check. Wardrobe change? Check."

"Barf bag?" said Ollie, holding up a small pink gift bag.

"You're not helping," Mimi scolded.

"It's not really a barf bag," said Max, as Ollie handed the present to Lark. "It's a little something from Ollie and me. To let you know that we're up on the stage with you in spirit."

Hands shaking, Lark reached into the bag beneath the tissue paper and removed her gift—a tiny pin of the British flag.

"Guys! This is so sweet." Lark handed the pin to Mimi, who fastened it to Lark's sweater. "Thanks. I love it."

"Knock 'em dead, kid!" said Ollie. "You're gonna be great!"

Then Mrs. Fitzpatrick was honking the horn in the driveway.

It was time to go!

CHAPTER TWENTY

According to the student-council members who were handing out programs at the door, this was shaping up to be one of the most highly attended talent shows Ronald Reagan Middle School had ever had.

"Just my luck," Lark had grumbled.

Mimi guided her to the dressing area backstage, gave her an encouraging high five, then went off to consult with the tech crew about loading up her video.

This left Lark and her guitar case alone with the ballerinas, the tuba players, the rhythmic gymnasts . . . and Howie Dornbaum, the magician. Her knees were shaking and her stomach felt like someone had fed her pterodactyls for lunch.

Principal Hardy, who was acting as emcee for the evening, was making her way to the stage.

This is it. Lark's heart began to rapidly beat in her chest.

"Hey. Great outfit."

She turned to see Teddy approaching across the dressing area. He looked flat-out adorable in his loose-fitting jeans, plain white T-shirt, and desert boots.

"Thanks," Lark managed to choke out. "You look good, too."

"Want to check out the competition from the wings?" he asked with a crooked grin. "See what we're up against?"

"Um . . . okay. Sure."

It took a moment to get her wobbly legs moving, but Lark picked up her guitar and followed Teddy down the hall to the stage entrance. Quietly, they positioned themselves in the shadows in time to hear the principal announcing the first act.

"Please give a warm welcome to Christina Li, who will be playing 'Ode to Joy' on the cello."

The crowd applauded as Christina took the stage, lit only by the soft glow of the footlights.

Her performance was flawless.

As the audience cheered, Lark peeked around the curtain to scan the sea of folding chairs. She gasped when she saw that every seat—stretching from the stage all the way to the back wall of the caf-a-gym-a-torium—was filled.

Make that *almost* every seat.

She spotted Max and Ollie sitting right next to Mimi's family in the third row. But next to them there appeared to be a gaping hole, a canyon of emptiness. Two unfilled seats.

213

She guessed that one of them belonged to one of Mimi's many aunts or uncles, who must have slipped out to use the restroom.

The second empty seat, of course, was her mother's.

Miserable, Lark stepped aside to allow Christina and her giant cello room to pass, then watched as the next act took the stage, dressed in gauzy harem pants and clacking finger cymbals.

"Please welcome the girls' intramural volleyball team," said Principal Hardy, "who will be performing a Bollywood-style dance routine." She smiled. "Or perhaps I should say Volley-wood?"

A smattering of laugher rippled through the crowd.

Unlike Christina's string solo, the dancers required more than just the footlights. When the spotlights went on, flooding the stage with dazzling glare, Lark could no longer see the audience.

The music swelled and the volleyball players began to stomp their feet.

"Not bad," said Teddy.

By the fifth act, Lark had decided that all middle school talent shows could be summed up in two words: "Who knew?"

For example, who knew that Dennis Breerly could yodel? Or that Samantha Pratt was an accomplished puppeteer? Who knew that Alex Waylon, sporting satin knee breeches and a three-corner hat, could recite the entire Declaration of Independence from memory? Mr. Saunders underscored the moment by playing a soft rendition of "The Star-Spangled Banner" on the piano. Unfortunately, the patriotic music only served to remind Lark about her Fourth of July fiasco . . .

"We're next," said Teddy. "How do you feel?"

Nauseated. Petrified. "Excellent!"

The stage crew set up a tall stool for Lark and a standing mike for Teddy.

"Now we'll hear from Teddy Reese, singing an original composition entitled 'Midnight,'" Principal Hardy announced. "He will be accompanied on guitar by Lark Campbell."

Lark stepped squinting onto the brightly lit stage and took her place on the stool. She heard Ollie and Max cheering, but the glare of the spotlights made it impossible to see if perhaps, by some miracle, her mother had arrived during the previous performance. The audience just looked like a massive, writhing silhouette without discernable faces.

Terror welled up and Lark's whole body trembled.

I want to go home.

She closed her eyes.

But it wasn't an auditorium filled with underwear-clad strangers she envisioned behind her eyelids. It was her tiny backyard in Tennessee, with the slanted swing set and the rosebay rhododendron sprouting blooms like pink ruffles on a little girl's party dress. She saw her old bike propped against the dogwood tree. She saw dew on the grass and a skittering of clouds over the distant hilltops.

The peacefulness of the memory calmed her.

Her fingers settled themselves on the strings.

Just. Play.

Lark strummed, and the notes of Teddy's song—which, thanks to their collaboration, had gone from being really good to beyond excellent—rose out of her instrument like mist billowing over the Smoky Mountains. Music filled the air as Teddy began to sing. When he reached the refrain, she heard her own voice, clear and confident, blending with his.

When Teddy finished singing, the crowd exploded into shouts and cheers.

The performance had been perfect. Lark had managed to stay conscious. And Teddy had just proved that he had more than enough talent to make Abbey Road whole again.

The problem was that Donna hadn't been there to see it.

In the wings, Teddy caught Lark in a hug and spun her around. "You were incredible!"

"No, *you* were! You were amazing."

Teddy laughed. "Thanks. But I couldn't have done it without you, Lark. It's over now, so you can relax and enjoy." He eyed the stage, where a sixth-grade boy was making horrible noises on a bagpipe. "Well, you can enjoy whatever *that* is!"

"Actually," said Lark, "it's not over. I signed up to sing a solo. I'm the last act."

"Seriously? You're going to sing?"

"That's the plan."

"I'm really impressed." His eyes searched hers. "What made you brave enough to face your fears like this?"

"You," Lark answered truthfully. "I wanted my mother to hear you sing because . . . because I thought you would be the perfect person to replace Aidan in Abbey Road. Telling her I was going to sing solo was the only way I could convince her to come to the show."

Teddy stared at her. "So you're going out there to do the thing that scares you most in the whole world . . . for me?"

Lark nodded. "For you . . . for the boys . . . and especially for my mom. Abbey Road means so much to her, and I couldn't stand to see it fail. I know she just needs to see you perform to realize you've got the talent and charisma to be the band's new keyboard player. But the only way I could get her to come to the show was to say that I was going to sing my song. You know, the one I showed you."

"'Is It Just Me?'"

"That's the one. But now I've gone and put myself in this

horrible situation for nothing because she isn't even here." Lark's voice caught and she struggled to keep the tears out of her eyes. "She didn't show up."

Teddy looked overwhelmed. "That's the most awesome thing anyone's ever done for me."

"Yeah, well . . ." Lark shook her head and sighed. "I guess it's true what they say. No good deed goes unpunished."

The bagpiper had finished piping and Howie the magician was preparing to pull a rabbit out of his hat. That meant Lark was up next.

"Can you hold this for me?" she said, thrusting her guitar into Teddy's hand.

Feeling sick to her stomach, she ran to the girls' dressing area, tugged off her sweater, changed into her faded jeans, and wriggled into her peasant blouse. Then she wrestled her hair into a loose up-do and flew back to the stage, putting the dangly earrings on as she ran.

Teddy was right where she'd left him, holding her guitar.

He did a double take when he saw her new look. "Wow! You look like a real country star."

Lark blushed. "I do?"

Onstage, Howie Dornbaum was finishing his magic act by putting Principal Hardy into a large cabinet and sawing her in half. This was a huge hit with the students in the audience.

"I wish he had one of those boxes where he could make someone disappear," Lark murmured. "I'd volunteer."

"Ladies and gentlemen," said Howie, "for my final illusion, I will put Principal Hardy back together."

Someone in the crowd called out, "Do you *have* to?" and everyone laughed.

Howie raised his arms and spoke an incantation. There was an enormous glittering puff of smoke and—presto! Principal Hardy stepped out of the cabinet, all in one piece.

Howie took his bow, then gathered up his top hat and the rabbit and left the stage.

Lark's knees buckled.

"And now, for our final performance of the evening," said Principal Hardy, "here is Lark Campbell, singing a song she wrote herself. Let's hear it for Lark!"

The crowd clapped politely, waiting for Lark to take the stage.

But Lark remained frozen in the wings.

At the mike, the principal frowned. "Lark Campbell," she repeated.

"Go on," Teddy urged. "You'll be great."

But Lark just shook her head. Her fingers were numb and her face felt as if it were on fire. "I can't. I just can't go out there all alone."

The applause faded to an awkward hush. Principal Hardy scowled into the wings and gestured anxiously for Lark to take the stage.

Still, Lark could not move. "I can't," she whispered to Teddy. "Oh, God, I feel like such a loser."

"Everyone does sometimes," Teddy whispered back. "Remember? Which is why you and I are going to sing your song . . . together."

To Lark's shock, Teddy reached out and took her hand. With a little tug, he guided her onto the stage.

Lark was glad for the glare of the lights. She didn't want to see the sneering expressions on those hundreds of faces in the audience.

"All you have to do is start playing," Teddy whispered. "I'm right here. I'll be singing with you, so just start—"

He was cut off by the loud squeal of the double doors opening at the far end of the auditorium. All heads swiveled to glower at the late arrivals.

Lark squinted into the glare, shading her eyes with her hand. She could just make out two figures, hurrying down the center aisle.

For a moment, she thought the spotlights had seriously altered her vision, because she could have sworn she was looking at . . .

Her dad!

It *was* him! He was following her mom as they skittered along the row of folding chairs to take their seats in the third row, next to Max and Ollie.

So the second empty seat didn't belong to one of Mimi's relations. Donna had reserved it for Jackson!

Lark's heart soared—just like a songbird.

She slid onto the stool and cradled her guitar.

Teddy grinned. "Okay, so, looks like you've got this. I'll leave you to it."

"No," said Lark. "Stay. Sing with me. Please?"

Teddy's answer was to sit down at the piano and count her in. "One, two . . . one, two, three four . . ."

And for the second time that night, Lark and Teddy filled the room with song. Behind them, Mimi's video montage was like a piece of moving art. The images faded in and out of one another . . . close-ups of Lark, smiling as she sang, strumming her guitar, swaying in time to the music, floating in the pool . . .

Is it just me, or do you feel this way, too?
I'm feeling so lost, like I don't have a clue.
Is it just me, thinking life's not on my side?
Is it just me, swimming against the tide?

The melody was sweet and the words were straight from the heart. Lark could feel every beat of it pulsing through her. When her eyes went to her parents, beaming with pride, she realized she had never been less afraid in her whole life.

When the song was over, the crowd rose to its feet to give the performers a standing ovation.

On the screen, the montage was ending with a slow-motion image of Lark, her back to the camera, walking toward the pink-and-gold clouds of a summer sunset. It lingered a moment, then faded to black as she and Teddy bowed once, then held hands and bowed again.

"Is this the best feeling in the world?" Lark shouted to him over the thunderous applause. "Or is it just me?"

"Oh, I'm pretty sure it's not just you," he shouted back.

Teddy and Lark moved upstage to allow the other acts to file out and take their final bows. Then Principal Hardy returned and waved her hands to get the audience to settle down.

It was time for the awards.

But as far as Lark was concerned, she'd already won.

CHAPTER
TWENTY-ONE

Lark zigzagged through the crush of families, classmates, and teachers. She replied with polite thank-yous to the people who called out congratulations as she hurried past, but she refused to stop or even slow down until she found who she was looking for.

She was so excited, she'd barely been able to listen as Principal Hardy announced the results of the competition. Teddy had to give her a nudge when their names were announced as the joint winning act for both the songs they performed together. Their prize was a gift certificate to Ice Cream Lab on Santa Monica Boulevard.

Then had come what was in Lark's opinion an even more thrilling announcement. The judges had been so impressed with Mimi's innovative video montage that they'd given her the runner-up award to honor the skill and sophistication of her work.

The minute Principal Hardy had dismissed the performers, Lark bolted from the stage on a mission.

"Songbird!"

"Daddy!" She doubled her pace, speeding toward her father to throw herself into his open arms.

"I've missed you so much!"

"I miss you too, baby girl."

He was holding her so tightly, she nearly couldn't breathe, and she was pretty sure she was crushing the bouquet of purple irises he'd brought, but she didn't care. "I can't believe you're here. And you know what? I don't even mind that scruffy beard of yours scratching my cheeks."

Jackson laughed. "I'm so sorry we missed your first song, darlin'. The plane was delayed."

"But you made it in time to hear 'Is It Just Me.' I fixed the bridge, the one you helped me with."

"It was perfect," said Jackson, placing her back on her feet and giving her a huge smile. "And the best part was that you got up there and sang it in front of all these people."

"I was shaking like a leaf."

"Couldn't tell from where I was sitting. You looked like a real pro."

Donna ran over to join them, wrapping her arms around Lark. "You! Were! *Amazing!* Oh, Lark, I am so proud! As my granny used to say, I am livin' in the high cotton tonight."

"Thanks, Mom."

"And you were absolutely right about Teddy," Donna continued. "He'd be a perfect addition to Abbey Road. I've already talked to Max and Ollie and they're all for it."

As if on cue, the boys appeared, looking somewhat frazzled.

"Y'all okay?" asked Lark.

Ollie laughed. "Never better. We got stopped to sign autographs."

"You brought the house down, Lark!" said Max. "You're a star. And speaking of stars . . . where's our boy Teddy? I want to shake his hand."

"Yes, where is Teddy?" asked Donna, shifting into professional mode. She began to scan the crowd. "The sooner I talk to him and his parents, the better. I wonder if they'd object to my stylist giving him a few blond highlights."

"Mom," said Lark with a giggle. "Slow down. You can have your people call his people in the morning."

"Of course. Sorry." Donna gave her a sheepish look. "You're right. Tonight is all about you, baby."

"Good. Then I vote we all go back home right now, where Dad and me can drink sweet tea and play our guitars under the stars."

Jackson's eyes turned serious. "Songbird, are you talking about Nashville? Because we've been over this and—"

"No, Daddy," Lark said, taking his hand. "I'm talking about my home right here in LA."

"Is that really how you feel?" asked Donna, her eyes shining, her voice hopeful.

Lark nodded. "I'm a lucky girl. I've got two places I can call home. After all, home is where the heart is . . . that's what people say."

"Hmm. Sounds like a great opening line for a hit, doesn't it?" Donna teased.

"Sure does!" Lark said, beaming. "It sure does."

Suddenly, someone was standing behind Lark, nervously clearing her throat. She turned to see Mimi, looking worried.

"Can I talk to you for a sec?" asked Mimi. "In private?"

"Sure, Meems." Lark excused herself and followed her friend to a quieter corner of the auditorium. "What's up?"

"This is what's up," said Mimi, holding out her cell phone. Paused on the screen was the "Homesick" music video. "As in *up*loaded . . . still."

It took Lark a moment to understand. "You mean the 'Homesick' video is still posted online? You never took it down?"

Mimi shook her head. "You know I only posted it so that you could show it to your mom that day you needed to prove that Aidan was lying." She shrugged. "But I sorta-kinda-oops forgot to take it down."

"So just take it down now. It's no big deal."

"Well, actually it *is* kind of a big deal. In fact, it's kind of a *huge* deal."

"Meems, what are you talkin' about? You're acting like a long-tailed cat in a room full of rocking chairs."

Mimi frowned. "Ohhh-kaayy . . . I have no idea what that means, but . . . look."

She pointed to the spot where the number of views was logged. Lark squinted at the tiny numerals and gasped.

"Mimi!"

"I know, I know!"

"*How?*"

"Best I can figure is that the footage I posted of Holly Rose with the boys got lots of views because she's a huge star. That sent people looking for other videos I've made. And, well . . . they found you." Mimi bit her lip. "Are you mad?"

Lark honestly did not know how to answer that. A day ago she would have been frantic about it. The thought of thousands of people hearing her sing her most intimate thoughts would have made her skin crawl. But tonight, everything had changed. She'd sung her original song in front of their entire school and won the talent show.

But winning a gift card to the Ice Cream Lab was a far cry from going viral in cyberspace.

"Do you want me to take it down?" Mimi asked, her finger poised over the phone's screen.

Lark opened her mouth to answer, but closed it again. What should she do? She had no idea. Should she leave the video posted for the entire world to see and enjoy or criticize? Or should she take it down immediately?

Was this her worst nightmare . . .

Or a dream come true?

Lark's singing is big news on YouTube.
But can she make it as a singer-songwriter –
and still be herself? Will she ever be
able to compete with the world's
hottest new boy band?

LOOK OUT FOR THE NEXT

GIRL
VS
BOY BAND

COMING SOON